Grumpy Billionaire's Baby Surprise

LILY CROSS

Contents

Chapter 1. Olivia

I'm lying in Jack's arms, my body still trembling from the intensity of our lovemaking.

My brother Paul's wedding isn't over yet, and I hear footsteps, cheerful chatter, and laughter in the corridor. People are already in the house. A twinge of nervousness comes over me, like a mouse smelling a cat.

"It's nothing. God knows how many men and women are going crazy behind every closed door now," Jack mutters. He turns over and lays on me again. Jack's eyes are piercing and full of intensity. His robust and chiseled body exudes power and confidence. As he looks at my face, my heart skips a beat.

It is the third time he has been on top of me since he dragged me into the room and closed the curtains.

Jack kisses my neck and shivers run down my spine. He's so strong and grumpy, even when we make love. But that's what I love about him—he's rough and passionate, and it makes me feel alive.

I kiss him back, exploring every inch of his body.

Jack doesn't know, and I do not want to tell him—it's my first time sleeping with a man. It's also the first time I've shown my love to the man I've dreamed of since I was a little girl. I have reserved myself for Jack for so long and want Jack to be himself with me.

Of course, I'm a little nervous, wondering what will happen next, but Jack makes me feel safe and loved.

As we continue, Jack becomes rough. His deep brown chest hair makes me think of a powerful monster. His muscular body presses against mine, and his fingers grasp my breasts like iron hooks. I began to feel tense and scared, and my pain has almost reached the limit, but it's overshadowed by the happiness I feel. Being with Jack is a dream come true, and I can't believe that it's finally happening.

I close my eyes, bearing his repeated impact, feeling all this to my heart's content in vertigo.

Afterwards, we lie in silence, our bodies intertwined. I can feel Jack's heart beating against mine, and I know that this is where I belong. I also know that Jack's rigid body hides a soft and kind heart.

I cup Jack's angular face in my hands, tenderness in my heart. This is a man I have loved since I was young. I remember.

One summer evening, Jack and my brother were leaving and spotted a feral black cat. The cat was about to ambush a little rabbit. Jack jumped for the little rabbit at the same time as the cat and scared the cat away. He held the little rabbit in his palms, stroking its fur. He could not hide the tenderness he felt. I fell in love with Jack at that moment.

"I love you," I whisper, breaking the silence.

Jack replies with a kiss, but no words.

We don't know how long we've been in bed. Light from outside filters between the curtains. Through the gap under the door, I see the hallway lights come on as well.

"Jack!" I hear my brother Paul calling.

Then I hear footsteps get closer and stop at the door, blocking the light. Someone knocks on the door.

"Jack, are you inside? An investor wants to meet you." Paul is still there, waiting for a response.

Jack is my brother's best friend; they helped each other as they grew up. My brother didn't forget to help Jack find investors, even at his wedding.

I stare at the door; I know my brother is still outside with a few others. The brown door is the only thing that covers my secret.

I hide under the covers. I know Paul has keys hidden above the doorframe.

It's hard to breathe under here.

Jack opens my cover and exposes me fully to his eyes.

"No one dares come in. Relax."

He confidently puts his arms under his head and speaks as if no one else is here. His voice is too loud, and I guess that my elder brother, the groom, must have heard it very clearly.

Jack is right.

Paul and the people outside the door whisper a few words and leave. I pray that my brother won't be looking for me in the crowd and will never find out that I'm the one with Jack.

The corridor is quiet again, and music comes in from the window. People outside start dancing again.

I look at the man resting beside me. He's been my crush since I was a little girl, and I always dreamed of being with him, but he never gave me a second look.

My brother's wedding allowed me to be close to him. When the music started, he walked towards me, smiling for the first time. We spun together on the green lawn; his smile removed my last line of defense. We slipped into the guest room together...

"I love you," I say, tears streaming down my face. I can't believe that I finally have Jack, the man of my dreams.

Jack dries my tears and says, "Don't repeat it. You deserve a better man."

But even as I revel in our love, I know that there will be challenges ahead. Jack is a grumpy and stubborn man, and we will clash in the future. For now, I'm content to bask in the afterglow of our lovemaking and let the future take care of itself. I will keep my future in my hands.

I drift off to sleep.

The following morning, I wake up to an empty bed, and my heart sinks. Jack is gone. I knew that he wouldn't stay the night, but it still hurts. I pull our pillows, check the end tables, open all the drawers, I hope I can find his note.

Nothing.

Jack disappeared entirely, as if he had never been here at all.

I dress and head downstairs, hoping to catch a glimpse of him before he leaves. But he's already gone.

I try not to let it get to me, but it's hard. After such a steamy night, he should at least give me a warm goodbye. but instead, he doesn't care.

My brother Paul and his new wife are already gone on their honeymoon to France.

The out-of-town guests are still here. It's my job to take care of them. I started preparing coffee in the kitchen. Breakfast will be here shortly.

The sun shines brightly. The coffee exudes a rich and mellow aroma. When changing the water for the flowers, I can still feel the aftermath of last night's tryst in many parts of my body, and my heart is already lamenting the loss.

As the day wears on, I try to keep myself busy with all the guests. I go shopping with two ladies, collect flowers for an old couple, and even try to focus on my acting work. But nothing seems to shake off the feeling of disappointment and heartbreak.

When night arrives, all the visitors are gone. I can hear my own lonely footsteps and I wander dazed through the big empty house.

The washer and dryer are running, and all the guests' bedding and bath towels are clean, but I don't bother to clean anything Jack touched.

It's late at night, and I don't want to return to my guest room, so I return to Jack's room like a ghost.

I turn off the lights, lie in bed alone, and reminisce about everything that happened last night.

Jack's pillow still smells faintly of his pomade. The smell of the perfume he used is still firm on the sheets. I stretch my arm to the other side of the bed, where Jack was lying. How I wish he were still there, within my reach.

I keep replaying our night together in my head, wondering if I did something wrong.

Did I give him the wrong impression?

Why did he leave without a word?

But deep down, I know that it's not my fault. Jack just isn't the commitment type. He's a lonely, tough guy who clings to his free soul, and I should have known that.

***

As the days turn into weeks, I try to move on. But it's hard. Every time I imagine seeing Jack again, I feel a pang of hurt and longing.

I know that I can't force him to commit. If he wants to be with me, he'll make it known. And if not, then I should take the challenge and bring him back to me. But until then, I'll focus on being the best version of myself and living my life to the fullest. One day Jack will come around and see that we're meant to be together.

With a mixture of sweetness and sadness, I step back into the studio. I'm here to audition for the role of a female soldier in the Middle East. It's a dream role for me, and I've been expecting it for months.

The audition room for the test shots is elementary, like an empty factory building. Behind a long row of desks sit a few men and women with stern faces. I can feel their eyes on me, judging me. Several cameras have been set up, aimed at the middle of the room from various angles. That's where I'm going to take the screen test.

I'm nervous, to say the least. I'm a novice, with no advantage compared to the movie stars who come in and out of the set. But I know that I must give it my all.

I take a deep breath and step forward, my heart pounding in my chest.

One of the directors gives me a brief overview of the scene. "Two minutes, you have two minutes to prepare," he tells me when he hands me the script. I put on my gear and feel like a real soldier. I try to embody the strength and courage that this character represents.

As I start the scene, I can feel the adrenaline pumping through my veins. I give it my all, trying to make every moment count.

When the scene ends, I feel both relief and exhaustion. I know that I gave it everything I had, but I'm not sure if it was enough.

Alex, the director, nods, and I can see a hint of a smile playing at the corners of his mouth.

"You did well," he says, his voice calm and measured. "But we still have more tests to run. We'll let you know." Alex is a good director with an easygoing disposition. He's like an old man who lives next door. His usual clothes are jeans and brightly colored T-shirts. But at this moment, he is severe enough to be intimidating.

I nod, feeling a mixture of hope and fear. I sleepwalk outside, taking deep breaths of fresh air, hoping to get the nod. I was the top student in all schools I attended, Now, I want to be one of the best actresses.

The next day, I get a call from the studio. It's from the director, Alex; I got the role. I'm ecstatic. It's my first feature film. But at the same time, I'm scared.

What if I fail?

What if I risk the investor's money?

Soon I get busy, and I have no time to worry. As the crew starts the pre-production process, I study the script, reading over each line. I lift weights and practice my lines in the mirror daily to be a good fit for the role.

I started running and exercising every morning. Initially, I could only sprint about fifty yards. Now I can run three hundred yards.

There's a morning breeze and I'm so happy. I know I can climb and run on the yellow mountain like the soldiers in the script. I've trained so hard to get ready for this shoot. Now I'm ready.

Just then, my cell phone rings. It's Alex, the director.

I stop and ask breathlessly, "What's the matter?"

"Are you running?" he asks, sounding urgent.

"Yes." I wonder why he asked. I run every morning and he knows it.

"I need you at the set for a meeting with the producer in two hours." Alex's says sternly.

"What's going on?" I ask.

"Go meet the producer," says Alex.

"Okay. I'm just going to finish my run."

"Olivia, stop. Go home at once and get ready to meet the new producer. You must be at your best."

"You sound like I'll be meeting the president," I joke.

"More serious than meeting the president. The president will turn around and forget you, and the new producer can kick you out."

I laugh. "A producer, is it that serious?"

"Olivia, this producer is extraordinary. A big name in our industry, known for being demanding."

"What's this guy's name?"

"Jack Freeman."

I can't laugh anymore. My heart beats faster than when I'm running. I lean on a tree, take deep breaths, then return home.

I shower, then begin to carefully groom myself. Accidentally, I turned the hair dryer to its highest setting, and before I know it, my hair is blown into a terrific mess, so I had to start again.

My features are well-defined, and I don't need heavy makeup. But I still need to figure out what to wear. I open the closet and take out an exquisite silver-gray suit with a skirt that makes my figure look stunning and slim. After I put it on, I stand in front of the mirror for a while and then take it off. Too formal, like the secretary of the boss of a big company. I put on a long evening gown, which looks elegant and luxurious, but more like something a wealthy lady would wear to a ball, making me look less energetic.

Suddenly, my fingers stop in front of a pink dress. This is what I wore to my brother's wedding. When dancing with Jack, its hem flowed against Jack's side. We haven't seen each other since that night of passion. This pink dress will remind him about the night we shared.

I put on a pink dress. I'm extremely excited as I drive to the office.

What will Jack feel when he sees me wearing this?

Chapter 2. Jack

The movie studio is excitedly buzzing as we begin pre-production on our latest film.

I sit comfortably in my chair and scan all the faces in the meeting room. The directors sitting solemnly wearing ties are the directors who know me.

As one of the top movie producers in Hollywood, I'm used to people calling me bossy. I don't care about any of the noise around me. All I care about is making great movies.

I've just taken over a pre-production movie and am here in the studio to meet all the critical people involved. The directors, production managers, and leading actors have gathered for this crucial meeting. Everything, no matter big or small, must be ready before a shoot. As a producer, I'm in charge of making sure everything runs smoothly.

I scan the meeting room and see Olivia walk in, wearing the same pink dress she had on the night of our one-night stand. My heart skips a beat.

Is she intentionally trying to cause trouble for me on the set? Is she trying to remind me of that night on purpose? I sense anger inside of me.

"Let's start," I say. My voice isn't loud, but the entire room becomes suddenly quiet.

The director starts presenting their vision for the film. He manages it well. I can feel my grumpy demeanor beginning to soften. They're passionate about the project, and I can't help but feel drawn in by their enthusiasm.

As the meeting continues, I notice one of the actresses in particular. Her name is Emily, and she's breathtakingly beautiful. Her piercing blue eyes and curly blonde hair are enough to make any man weak in the knees. But it's not just her looks that catch my attention: it's how she carries herself, with a quiet confidence that's alluring and intimidating. As we discuss the details of the film, I find myself drawn to Emily. Her input is intelligent and thoughtful, and I can tell that she's fully committed to the project. I can feel Olivia watching me throughout the meeting. The expression on her face keeps changing. I ignore her.

I must focus on the film and not let my personal feelings get in the way. I must act professionally; no love games should be played here.

I start reviewing the script with the directors, and I can see Olivia's passion for the project. She's fully committed to bringing her character to life, and I can't help but feel drawn to her energy as well. As we discuss the scenes, I notice how her sweet voice fills the room, and she also seems to enjoy herself very much. Unfortunately, as she's acting, she doesn't integrate herself into the character. Her voice is as gentle as a princess, without a soldier's decisiveness. I can't resist the urge to tease her.

"Your voice is too sweet, Olivia. You can sing on stage, but you don't sound like a soldier," I say, a grin on my face.

"I don't think so," she replies, rolling her eyes. "I don't want to make audiences deaf."

As I watch Olivia, I notice one problem with the new film. She just doesn't fit the leading role. Her voice is too sweet, too innocent for the character.

Alex, the director, is sitting next to me; he turns to me partway through. "She's wonderful, isn't she?" he compliments unabashedly, his face full of satisfaction.

The assistant director nods approvingly. She tells me in a muffled voice, "To adapt to the role's needs, Olivia is doing physical exercise daily."

I smile calmly. "Unfortunately, Olivia is just a beautiful ceramic doll without the attitude of a soldier."

I know I must make a tough decision.

"Change the lead actress," I say, turning to the director.

"What?" The director can't believe what I've said.

"Jack wants you to change the lead actress. He doesn't like Olivia," the assistant director whispers to Alex carefully, while glancing at me.

"Are you sure?" the director questions, surprised.

"Yes," I confirm.

"Why?" the director asks loudly.

"She's not a good fit." I throw the script on the desk. My voice can be heard by everyone in the room. The entire room goes quiet.

Olivia stands in the middle of the room, her mouth open, and her face turns red.

"Let Emily take the lead. She has a better understanding of the script. She's a better fit." My voice is firm.

"Listen up, everyone," I bark, my voice gruff and no-nonsense. "We need to talk about the lead actress for this film." The others all look at me, their eyes filling with curiosity. "I don't think Olivia is right for the role," I say, my voice popping with frustration. I cross my leg and continue, "Her image just doesn't fit the personality of a female soldier. We need someone with more muscle who can run as fast as a male soldier on the battlefield."

"But, sir," one of the directors starts to protest. "Olivia has already been in the cast. She has been exercising ridiculously hard every day."

I see the others nod. Olivia must be a favorite person here. Everyone likes her except Emily, Olivia's competitor.

"She's perfect for the role of Cinderella in the pumpkin cart scene." I don't even look at that director who calls me sir, not my name, Jack.

"It is not fair," one actor says from the back row.

"We need someone who looks like they can handle themselves in a war zone. Olivia looks so frail like she could be broken by a gust of wind," I snap. The directors all exchange worried glances, but I know I'm right. Making a movie is a business, and I must make the best decisions for the film. I sit back and continue, my voice low and serious. "I want a girl with a big ass and muscular calves. Someone who can kick ass and take names."

Alex leans to me and asks, "Jack, can we discuss our budget first? We've got time. We can discuss changing roles later."

"Change the lead actress now. That's my decision, this is not a negotiation."

The directors nod in agreement, and I know we're one step closer to creating something unique.

Good!

I stand up and leave. I have another meeting I need to attend shortly.

As I walk to the parking lot. I can't help but think about Olivia. I know I must've hurt her by removing her from the lead role.

"Jack!" I hear a sad voice calling my name.

I stop, turn, and see Olivia running behind me.

She's running on the path among the green bushes, her pink dress fluttering in the breeze, and she looks like a beautiful elf. But her face is sad.

Olivia catches me. She breathes hard, then looks up at me with a mixture of anger and hurt in her eyes.

"Why did you do this?" she asks, her voice trembling. I look into her eyes without reply.

"Why did you take me out of the lead role?" she keeps asking.

"I did it because I thought it was best for the film," I say, my voice full of frustration. "I know it hurt you, but I had to make a tough decision."

"But you could have talked to me about it," she says, tears welling in her eyes. "We could have figured something out together."

"A producer does not need to get permission from an actress." I move closer to her. "Olivia, I do not have to figure out business with your input. I make my own decisions."

"At least you should let me try. If you give me a chance, we can work this out," Olivia insists.

"There is no 'we' here. Just a producer and an actress. Understand?" My tone has become angrier.

"Jack, I thought you were my brother's best friend. Not just a producer," she says, raising her voice a little.

"I'm still your brother's best friend. But friendship cannot make a movie." I see a few people walking in our direction. I lower my voice. "You can't expect me to treat you as special just because I'm your brother's friend. Making a movie is a business, and I must make the best decisions for the film."

"You're so wrong. I don't expect any favoritism from you. But treat me fairly and with respect."

"I know you always want to be the best. But, if you start on the wrong foot, you can only be a rock, not a star."

"We had—" Her face turns shy.

When Olivia says this, she doesn't notice the people behind her getting closer. I wave to a the few who are closest and call "Hi," insincerely. Fortunately, Olivia stops her speech in time and doesn't continue to expose our secrets.

However, she starts chattering again when those people have just walked away.

Shyly she mutters, "We had one steamy night—"

"A night... I fucked you and fucked you good," I interrupt her with anger. How dare she try to mix business and personal relationships together. "Olivia," I say, frustrated. "We need to talk."

She looks up at me, her sweet face filled with sadness.

"The audience wouldn't buy it if you play the lead. And you also shouldn't remind me about the one-night stand while we're at the studio." I look into her eyes, and her sad face makes me feel bad, but I must make it very clear. "It's unprofessional. It makes it difficult for me to work with you."

Olivia lowers her head. Her face turns pale white. I can feel my heart softening as I look at her. Despite our past, I can't help but feel drawn to her.

"Listen," I say, my voice barely above a whisper. "Making a movie is a tricky business. I must concentrate. I focus only on making a good movie whenever I step into the studio. If you want to work with me, we have to always be professional, even if it's difficult. I know it's not easy, but it's the only way."

"I didn't mean to cause any trouble," she says. Tears are rolling down her beautiful face. "I just wanted to be a successful actress and be close to you too," Olivia says quietly.

"Olivia, remember, nothing personal between us here." She is harassing me. I can't explain more clearly than I've just done.

"Jack, I've been missing you—"

Stop it. Don't look back. I must turn her down. She's brilliant but too young to know how deep the business world is. She could cause me a big problem without even knowing it. "We can't do this."

Olivia does not answer. A pained expression appears on her face.

I often deal with handsome men and beautiful women. These actors and actresses can instantly change their expressions from immense joy to great sorrow. However, I know that at this moment, her pain is not a show but an expression of her heart.

She had been expecting to be in the lead actress position for a long time. She had been trying hard to make herself fit that role. When I removed her from the lead, I was the one who damaged her dream.

But removing her from the lead role is not only a responsible choice for the business but also a way to help her. If her first film loses money, she won't have another chance.

"Olivia, please don't feel too bad. There will be a role that fits you better and leads you to success."

I don't want to hurt her more than I have. She nods, and for a moment, I can see a glimmer of hope in her eyes. I could still find her role in this film. That is the deal. I'll make this work. Olivia can play a nurse or an operator.

I call Alex, the director. "We need to find a role for Olivia in the script. Keep her in the film."

Alex's voice is happily surprised. "Absolutely! I'm on it. Any suggestions?"

I glance at Olivia; she's trying to listen. I say, "Nope. You decide. Just make sure it's a good fit for her."

Alex replies without hesitation, having already thought about it before receiving my call. "I have some ideas for Olivia's role. How about a supporting character who helps the protagonist in a crucial moment?"

"Sounds good to me. What do you think, Olivia?" I ask, turning to her.

Olivia jumps and yells, "I love it! That sounds like an exciting role."

The director laughs loudly, "Great! I'll get to work on the script revisions."

"And keep me in the loop," I add.

"Of course, Boss. You'll be the first to see the new script."

I remind the director, "Good. And make it fast. We have a tight schedule."

Alex replies firmly, "No problem. I'll have it done by the end of the week."

When I finish the conversation, I see Olivia smile again.

I rush to another meeting. I know Olivia must be watching as I leave. But I don't look back.

My driver takes us along the tree-lined road. The vehicle's window occasionally flashes a glimpse of the branches, just like the scene of having a good relationship with Olivia keeps flashing through my mind.

I can't help but recall our night together. I'm no stranger to women. Beautiful, intelligent, versatile, lousy character, notorious, greedy, and shameless—I have dealt with them all. If I write down the names of all the women I've slept with, that list would be awfully long.

Olivia is unique. She's too pure at heart for Hollywood. I sigh.

I've seen it happen before. One mistake, one misstep, and everything can come crashing down. I can't let someone like Olivia ruin it for me. I've worked too hard to get where I am now.

I should avoid her as much as possible. It doesn't matter if she finds a way to cross my path or comes into my office with smiles and giggles, even undresses herself in front of me again... I should not encourage her.

That's it. Never touch Olivia, and never be touched by Olivia.

Chapter 3. Olivia

I watch as Jack strides farther and farther away. I hope he'll look back, but he doesn't.

Why was Jack so angry with me today?

Have I done something wrong?

My head is empty. I'm still in shock. I can't think of anything.

It's a lovely day, but I'm so sad. I've put so much effort and dedication into this role, only for it to be taken away from me by the man I love.

And then it hits me—I'm still wearing the same pink dress I had worn on the night Jack and I had our steamy encounter.

Is that the reason for his anger?

Is he trying to protect himself by pushing me away?

I can feel my anger rising, replacing the sadness.

It's not fair.

I shouldn't have to suffer because of something that happened between us.

Lost in thought, I hear a voice calling my name as I sit there. "Hey, you okay?" It's from my best friend, Sarah. She's only in two scenes as an operator, so she wasn't invited to the meeting.

"No, I'm not okay," I say, my voice shaking with emotion. "Jack took the role away from me."

"What? Who is Jack? Why?" Sarah asks incredulously.

"Jack is the new producer," I say, tears welling in my eyes. "He just said I wasn't right for the part and gave it to someone else."

"Who'd he give it to?"

"Emily," I reply. I can see Emily's happy face still.

"That's ridiculous," Sarah says, putting her arm around me. "You're perfect for that role, and you know it."

"Right," I agree. I know I'm a much better actress than Emily.

"Don't let Emily beat you. She isn't a nice person." Sarah puts her hands on my shoulders.

I nod. I cannot agree with what Jack just told me. I should be the star, not the rock; without an opportunity, how could I approve?

"You can fight back," Sarah says, her eyes sparkling with determination. "Confront the producer, demand an explanation, and don't take no for an answer."

I get up from the bench, wiping away my tears. "I can do this," I say, feeling stronger already.

I return to the studio, I grab a coffee and head to my dressing room, trying to gather my thoughts and figure out what to do next.

As I enter the room, I see Emily, the actress who has taken my place, reading the script with a smile. She looks up and sees me, and her smile only widens.

Why Emily is here?

"Oh, hi!" she says, practically bouncing out of her seat. "I'm so excited to be playing the lead role. It's such an amazing opportunity, the producer must like me very much, don't you think?"

I clench my jaw, feeling a wave of jealousy wash over me. Emily had always been friendly to me, but now I can't help but see her as my enemy, the person who had taken away the role I had worked so hard for. She may also try to get Jack next.

"Yeah," I say, my voice flat.

Emily doesn't notice my tone. "I just can't believe it," she says, still beaming. "I mean, I knew I had a chance, but I never thought I'd get it. And now I get to work with Jack and all these amazing actors. It's a dream come true."

Oh, Jack. Jack, your name is a rock that hits my heart. I hear his name again, but this time it's from Emily, who is heartless about all my feelings.

"Good luck." I nod, trying to keep my emotions in check.

It's not Emily's fault. She didn't know what had happened between Jack and me.

But still, it hurts to see her so happy and proud in front of me, knowing that I've lost everything.

As Emily continues to gush about the role, I can feel myself getting angrier and angrier. I want to lash out at her and tell her that she doesn't deserve it, but I know that won't solve anything.

Instead, I take a deep breath and focus on what I can do next.

I need to talk to Jack and figure out why he has taken the role away from me. There may be a chance for me to get it back.

I can't watch Emily's behavior anymore. I stand up and walk to the dining hall.

As I sit down to have my lunch, I can't help but notice the other actresses eyeing me up and down. I'm wearing a pink dress, which is drawing some attention.

"Your dress is so pretty," one of them says, smiling at me.

I smile back, feeling a little self-conscious. "Thanks," I say, trying to be polite. But then Emily walks by. She followed me to the dining hall. My mood immediately changes.

"Not a good fit," she mutters, loud enough for me to hear.

I feel a surge of anger. "What's that supposed to mean?" I say, my voice rising.

Emily turns to face me, a smug expression on her face. "Just that the dress isn't your style, is it?" Her voice is dripping with condescension. "It's more of a summer dress, and it's spring right now."

How dare she talk to me like that? But then I realize that "Not a good fit" are the words Jack used when he removed me from the lead actress position. I stare at Emily. Is this some kind of sick joke? Just a few hours ago, she was the one who tried to please me in many ways. I can feel my face getting red with anger.

"Don't worry. The director, Alex, likes you," Emily says, smiling. "Alex may find you a role, so you can play Cinderella in the pumpkin cart," Emily said, mimicking Jack's tone, then laughs loudly. Everyone around can hear her words.

"You know what?" I say, my voice shakes with emotion. "I don't care what you say. And I certainly don't care what Jack thinks. I'm a good fit for that role. At the very least, I'm a much better fit than you." The other people look at me and are surprised, but I don't care. This is my first time arguing with the others in the studio. I'm tired of being pushed around, and I won't take it anymore. With a determined look, I grab my lunch and head out of the dining hall, ready to take on whatever challenges come my way.

As I walk down the hallway, I can feel my confidence growing.

I could still get the lead actress role back.

Jack is somewhere else, in another meeting by now. I can convince the director that I'm the right person for the job. With that in mind, I head to Alex's office.

When I get there, Alex is on the phone, but he sees me and nods, acknowledging my presence. He finishes his conversation quickly, then greets me warmly, but I can tell from his expression that something is off.

"I'm sorry about what happened," Alex says, gesturing for me to sit down. "I'm sorry, but Jack made the final decision. Emily is the new lead actress."

I know I was wrong. I shouldn't look for help from Alex. Alex is a nice guy, but he will not dare to challenge Jack to help me. It would not be wise. I feel a pang of disappointment, but I try to stay positive.

"That's okay," I say, trying to keep the disappointment out of my voice. "Is there any other role I could play?" I ask.

Alex nods, pulling out a script from his desk. "Yes. It's not as big as the lead, but it's still a great part. And I think you'd be perfect for it."

Alex hands me the script, and I start reading the lines he's already marked for me. As I go on, I can feel my excitement waning. The role is nothing like the lead—it's a minor supporting character with only a few lines. It's a new addition roughed into the script for me. This role just can't compare to what I had been hoping for.

"I appreciate the offer," I say, trying to steady my voice. "But I'm really hoping for something more substantial. Is there anything else?"

Alex looks at me sympathetically. "I'm sorry," he says. "But this is the only other role available right now. I wish I could offer you more, but my hands are tied."

I nod, feeling defeated. "Okay," I say, standing up. "Thank you for considering me." I get ready to leave Alex's office.

Alex calls out to me.

"Wait," he says, his voice low. "There's one other option. It's not a big part, but it's important."

I feel a flicker of hope in my chest. This may be my chance to show what I'm capable of. "What is it?" I ask, feeling a sense of excitement building.

"It's the operator role," Alex says, handing me the script again. "It's not a huge part, but it's still important to the story. And I think you could do it justice."

When Alex suggested giving me a different role, I felt a sense of hope building inside me. But when he mentions the operator role, I feel conflicted.

"No," I say hesitantly. "That's Sarah's role. I don't want to take it away from her."

Alex nods understandingly. "I get how you feel," he says, "but sometimes, things don't go as planned in this business. And I think Sarah would understand if we gave you the role instead."

"But I can't do this," I decide. I know what it feels like to have a role taken away from you. I can't do that to Sarah. I'm ready to leave.

"Wait. Let me call Jack." Alex starts dialing. Alex doesn't give up on me. He is trying to convince Jack to give me the lead role back. My heart feels warm.

"No answer," Alex says and starts texting. "I texted him a message. He'll call back. Wait here."

I know Jack is in the meeting now. He's not able to answer calls or text messages. As we wait for Jack's call, Alex returns to work. I turn and look out the window, feeling my nerves building. This is my last chance to get back my lead role. I want to show Jack I'm capable of playing this part. But what if he says no?

As time goes by, I start to feel increasingly nervous. What if this doesn't work out? What if I never get the chance to play a lead role again? What if Jack thinks I'm the troublemaker? What if I push Jack away from me? So many what-ifs are tumbling through my mind. But then, just as I'm about to give up hope, Alex's phone rings.

"It's Jack," he says, looking excited. "He's calling me back."

I can feel my heart pounding as Alex answers the phone.

"Hey, Jack," Alex says, his voice low. "Listen, Boss, I want to talk to you about the lead role. Olivia is the best person for the job."

"Alex." Jack's voice booms through the phone. "What makes you think so?" It's clear he's in a bad mood. He sounds like he doesn't want to be bothered.

Alex tries to reason with him, but Jack is having none of it. "No," he says firmly. "She's not playing the lead. End of story."

I can feel a sense of disappointment washing over me. This was my last chance to prove myself, but now it feels like it's slipping away.

"But, Jack," Alex tries again, his voice pleading, "she's worked so hard. And she's talented. I think she could do a fantastic job."

Jack's voice is cold and dismissive. "I don't care how hard she's worked," he says. "She's not playing the lead. That's final."

As I listen to Jack's voice, I can feel a sense of anger building inside me. How could Jack be so dismissive? Didn't he see how much this meant to me?

But then, as Alex tries to reason with him again, I have an idea. There may be a way to change Jack's mind.

"Can I talk to him?" I say, my voice shaking a little. "Maybe I can convince him." My voice is quiet. I don't want Jack to hear it.

Alex looks surprised, but then he nods. "Sure," he says, handing me the phone.

I take a deep breath, trying to steady my nerves. "Jack?" I say tentatively. "It's me. Look, I know you don't want to give me the lead role. But I promise I can do an excellent job. Just give me a chance."

There's a long pause on the other end of the line, and I can hear Jack breathing heavily.

His heavy breath reminds me of the night he was on top of me. I hate to think about this. It just automatically comes to my mind. All my memories about the night with Jack. His heavy breath, his strong hands, his rough touch. Even during that moment, he was not gentle with me. He was wild like a beast on the bed, and now, he is a bossy alpha male in the studio.

"I've made my decision," he says, his voice gruff. "You're not playing the lead. That's it."

No way to change Jack's mind. He is so grumpy and bossy. I turn off the phone and hand it back to Alex.

"Olivia, don't cry. I can modify the script and create a better role for you." Alex stands up. He's upset too, but he still wants to help me out. It would be wonderful if Alex could make it happen, but how will that affect the entire crew's pre-production work? It will slow down everything, and many pieces will have to be changed.

"No, that would cause a delay on the shooting schedule." I smile through tears. "Thank you, Alex. You are an exceptionally good director. You've done more than enough for me."

I leave with tears rolling down my face. I get into my car and call my brother, Paul, who has just returned from his honeymoon.

"Hey, Sis." When I hear Paul's voice, I start crying again. "What's going on?"

"It's Jack. He removed me from the lead role, and now, I'm out of that film."

Paul doesn't reply. The only thing I can hear is his deep breath. Finally, he says, "He must have a reason." Paul still trusts his friend.

"He said I'm not a good fit. That I can only play Cinderella. He embarrassed me in front of all the directors. How could he do this to me?"

"Olivia, what do you want me to do?"

"Nothing, I just need someone I can talk to."

"Olivia, I'm a developer, not a filmmaker. I can turn a farmer's vast land into a city, but I know nothing about making a movie." Paul sighs, "I wish I could help you more." Paul's voice is more like a businessman, not a brother.

I hang up the phone. Paul keeps calling me back, but I don't want to answer. It was a mistake to call him, and I regret it. I must fight my way out on my own.

I start the car and head to my apartment. This is the end of my love for Jack, I tell myself.

Chapter 4. Jack

I walk onto the studio set, looking for Olivia before anything else. Soon I find her. She's sitting on a bench under a tree, looking sad and lost.

I got a call from Paul a few days ago. He's worried about his little sister. Paul had hoped I could guide Olivia to become a good actress, but he didn't ask for any favors. Paul knows me very well; we've always had mutual respect and trust.

I watch as Olivia sits there lonely; I don't feel guilty. Instead, I feel disappointed in her. If she gets so tied into knots for not getting a role, she'd better pack her bags and leave Hollywood. She can go to McDonald's and make French fries or wear a miniskirt and work as a front desk secretary somewhere. Hollywood has zero tolerance for the weak.

Removing her from the lead role is a business decision. It's also a decision to protect her future development. In a business, you can't let emotion guide decisions.

"Olivia," I say, approaching her tentatively. "How are you doing?"

She glares at me. "Why do you care?" she asks, her voice laced with bitterness.

I sigh. There's no easy answer.

"I know you're hurt," I say. "But it's not personal. You're just not a good fit for that lead role."

She snorts, looking away from me. "That's what *you* say," she mutters under her breath.

I've tried to reason with her. Every time I tried to talk to her, she shuts me down. It's the same today. In her eyes, we're enemies now. It's not a big deal to me. I understand that her original crew goes out to shoot, leaving her alone with nothing to do but audition. She may feel left out. But Olivia is overreacting. She is a grown woman, not a bratty yellow-haired girl anymore.

If she knows how to fuck, she should also know how to behave like an adult. I drop a script and a casting call on the bench next to her.

"Olivia," I say. "I heard about this audition. I think you'd be great for the lead."

She takes a long pause, but I don't have the patience to make her happy, so I turn to leave.

"Why are you doing this?" Her voice trembling.

"Take it or leave it," I say. "It's your decision." I fall silent.

There's another pause, and I hear her say from behind, "Okay. I'll think about it."

I attend the audition two days later.

More than a hundred young actresses are there. Some walk on the green field outside to get a little relaxation before their turn.

I watch through the camera nervously as Olivia takes the stage. The competition is high. I hope she wins. As Olivia starts to perform, I feel myself holding my breath. I hide my feelings, acting like I don't know her.

When she finishes her performance, there's a long moment of silence. And then, slowly but surely, the room erupts into applause. This almost never happens during an audition.

Olivia bows politely, then leaves.

At sundown, the first round of auditions concludes, and we must choose two actresses for the final audition. Each girl is great in her own way. I cherry-pick Olivia; then she becomes one of the two finalists. I stand up and walk out of the room. I'm so happy for Olivia from the bottom of my heart, and I cannot show it in front of the others.

The crowd outside has dispersed, only a dozen or so hopefuls sitting in a row of chairs anxiously awaiting the result. Olivia isn't there. I know where Olivia could be. I must tell her the good news.

I head to the water fountain and sure enough, I see her. She is looking at the sunset clouds in the west. Her back looks unbelievably beautiful. In the sauce vat of Hollywood, Olivia should be a pure and clean porcelain doll. I hope she won't rot in this huge sauce jar once she becomes famous someday.

I stand in front of Olivia. She pretends I'm invisible. What a proud girl. A huge grin spreads across my face. "You did it." She looks at me as if we've never met. I say, "You nailed it." Her body moves a little. She wants to stand up facing me. But she doesn't. "You're one of two for the final audition," I say more clearly.

Her eyes fill with uncertainty. "But what if I don't get the part?" she asks.

I put a hand on her shoulder. "You will," I say, my voice firm. "I believe in you."

Excitement flashes quickly in her clear eyes, but it's replaced by silence. She quietly watches the sunset in the distance and sits there without saying a word.

It is the first time I feel sorry for her.

"How will you win the role?" I ask.

Olivia stands up and looks into my eyes, "Forgetting who I am, merge myself with the character." Her voice is determined. Then she turns and returns to the studio.

I have no time to attend the final audition, but a day later, I receive a call from Olivia's brother Paul.

"Jack, Olivia made it." Paul is excited. He tells me Olivia passed the audition and got the lead role.

I'm so proud of Olivia. I feel an indescribable relief. I'm even happier than Paul. I can see Olivia having success with this film. Her innate elegant temperament, graceful movements, and intelligent eyes are perfect for this role.

So, that evening, I invite Olivia out to celebrate in a high-end restaurant, surrounded by the glitz and glamour of Hollywood.

The environment is full of romance. It feels like old times again. Olivia is wearing a black evening dress with a low cut and strapless shoulders. Her soft golden hair is tied behind her head, looking elegant and beautiful. But even as we laugh and talk, I can sense that something is still holding us back.

"Jack," Olivia says, looking at me seriously, "I don't know if I should dine out with you. It could be a mistake."

"Why not?" I push back.

"I just don't want to get hurt again." Her voice is low and severe.

"How can a dinner hurt you?" I joke back, making fun of her. "Would you drown yourself in a wine glass." I hold up my glass and keep joking. "Or choke on a steak?"

"It's not the food or drink. It's you. You're the one who can hurt me." Her voice is firm.

"I won't hurt you," I say, trying to reassure her.

"You did, and you will again." Olivia does not give up.

I sigh, feeling a sense of helplessness. It's not fun arguing with a woman. I shut up and simply focus on my meal.

"I want to be with you," Olivia says, looking at me seriously.

"I'm with you now," I say. I do not want to discuss this topic with her, seriously. I like women, but I don't want to make a commitment to any of them. "We can move the table away if you want to be closer." I glance at her.

My words work well as Olivia becomes quiet. I feel satisfied.

I order another dessert for myself. This restaurant offers the best ice cream in the world, but it's not something an actress should eat.

I look at Olivia. When she is quiet, she seems more like an angel. At this moment, she must be thinking deeply. It's a good thing for both of us, and I'm relieved.

"Jack," Olivia starts talking again, "I'm falling in love with you."

I drop my spoon onto the ice cream plate.

"Stop. Olivia." My mood suddenly changes to anger. "Listen, I make love with women, but I do not fall in love with anyone," I declare loudly. My voice is too loud, and it attracts the attention of our neighbors at the next table. They look our way. I don't care who they are or what they think. I must make my position clear to Olivia.

What I say obviously surprises her. She stares at me blankly with her beautiful eyes wide, a look of bewilderment.

"I need freedom. I cannot stand any constraints. I'll never get into the cage of marriage and let my creativity be destroyed. My rules are no commitment, no family, no children."

"I can wait," Olivia mutters quietly, but firmly.

"Then you must be very patient. Because you need to wait until the next life," I say.

"One day, you'll change your mind," she says softly, her head leaning to the side as she smiles up at me. There is confidence in her gentle eyes.

Seeing that Olivia is still so stubborn, I'm even angrier. "If you're lucky, don't wait until the next life. I can buy you a place by the cemetery."

"Let me buy you a place next to mine. I can't imagine many women will have a place beside your grave." She picks up the glass and drinks it all in one gulp. Soon, her face turns from pale to red. She looks at me with a flushed face and a challenge in her eyes. Her eyes are burning and compelling.

I stop talking to this sharp-mouthed girl and concentrate on eating.

After finishing my meal, I throw the white fabric napkin on the table. We leave and walk along the street. It's beautiful under the streetlights, and we stroll arm in arm. As we walk, I can feel the tension between us building once again. It has been so long since we have been this close, and I can't help but feel a sense of anticipation.

Finally, we find ourselves at a quiet bench facing the lake. It is a lovely and private spot, and I can feel my heart racing as I sit beside Olivia.

Olivia starts to talk about the new film, her voice low and serious.

I do not want to talk or listen.

I want to touch her.

She is wearing a low-cut black dress, and my hand drives straight into her plump breasts. I grab her soft nipple effortlessly. I squeeze it lightly, feeling the soft nipple harden between my fingers, then I move my hand to grab the other one. It's a tentative, gentle gesture at first, but then she starts to respond. And then we are kissing, our bodies pressed together in the darkness. It's a passionate, intense moment, and I can feel the chemistry between us building, robust and vital.

"Jack," she says, pulling away from me. "I don't know if this is a good idea."

"Why not?" I ask. I don't want to stop.

She hesitates, looking at me seriously. "I just don't want to get hurt again," she says.

"I won't hurt you," I say, my voice low and serious. I hug her, unzip her low-cut black dress, and unhook her black lace bra, exposing her firm breasts in the moonlight. They look so perfect. Petite nipples are adorable. I hold Olivia's breasts tightly, and the softness makes me feel the same tenderness.

I fear Olivia will stop me; however, she becomes like a docile cat, letting me play with her. I can do whatever I want. Her dress slips a little more, exposing her entire white upper body to the bright, full moonlight, her curves as beautiful as Venus.

I start to go crazy. Olivia's breasts kept changing shape under my grasp. I start kissing, from soft to rough, and I finally bite them with my teeth.

Under cover of night, I become crazier and crazier. I start taking off her dress completely.

Suddenly she grabs my fevered hands.

"Jack, can we go to the hotel?"

I pull away from her hands. I can't stop. My hands keep undressing her. My heart is burning with passion, and if I stop now and get a hotel room, I will be burned to the ground.

"Right here," I say.

"I have no promises or any commitment to you. Understand?" I loathe myself for speaking such callous words to my prey in the heat of desire.

"I understand, no commitment, no family, no children," she whispers, "but it's your rule, not mine."

"I can be rough. Once I get into a situation, I sometimes can be… thoughtless," I continue my warning.

Olivia does not reply.

"I might hurt you." I can't bear it. I've stripped her naked as I speak.

Under the moonlight, the lines of her body are so soft and beautiful, so exquisite that it is beyond words.

I know she is still nervous about the coming storm from her breathing, but she is ready to take what I will do to her.

When the storm is over, and I lie on top of Olivia to rest, I notice that I have left deep tooth marks on her full and firm breasts. Her nipples are also more prominent than they used to be, swollen from sucking so hard.

Olivia opens her eyes. She looks at me tenderly and smiles shyly.

"Jack." She calls my name softly; her fingers are in my hair.

My nerves suddenly tense, and I stare at her tightly. "Never tell me you love me, girl." I bite my lip to hold these words out of my mouth.

"Jack, you are a monster."

Looking at Olivia, I feel suspicion in my heart. Could it be that she is a masochist? Because few people can fully accept my misbehavior. Then I feel sorry. I was too aggressive with Olivia.

"Are you okay?" I ask. I am ready for any complaints from her.

Her response is a long kiss.

I kiss her back, and then I lift her from the bench. I carry her to the green field. The grass is softer than the bench.

"Do you want another one?" I ask.

Her reply is a sweet smile, and her hands are already on my back. Without a word, our bodies merge again.

This time, I'm more presumptuous and venting wholly and entirely. I close my eyes and concentrate on feeling the pleasure of each impact. I have never felt so full of passion before. I see Olivia's smile full of relief when the storm is over again. In the moonlight, her smile is very charming. I hold her tightly in my arms.

But I will not allow myself to fall in love with her.

Chapter 5. Olivia

The full moon glows in the sky, casting a soft light over the river. I can hear the gentle sound of the water and I breathe in the fresh, crisp air. I feel at peace. But my heart races with anticipation as I wait for Jack's touch.

In the moonlight, I see Jack's hairy chest again and feel his almost violent movements again, and when our bodies merge, I put my heart into his. This grumpy, rough man is unique and risky to get closer to. His hands and words can be painful at times. He does not just kiss; he bites and bites hard on the most sensitive parts of me. Even as his lust escalates, he keeps his sanity and warns me clearly, he can't give me any commitment. There is no future for us....

But I still love him.

I only need one commitment: the one I make to my heart.

I can't help the way I feel about him. I have loved him since I was a little girl. His every touch sends shivers down my spine, and I love him with all my heart. If there is no future, I will enjoy every second of now.

In this world, in this life, only Jack can touch me.

I feel Jack's arms around me, holding me closer. He is resting now.

He is still breathing deeply, his heart is beating violently, and he has not calmed down from the intense exertion. I brush his hair with my fingers, and his wise eyes smile. Even in the darkness, his eyes are so bright. How I wish that time would freeze at this moment, that we could have each other forever. Despite his gruff exterior, I know Jack is the one for me. I know he cares for me deeply, even if he won't admit it. He's not one for grand gestures or flowery words, but his actions speak louder than anything he could ever say.

Jack needs to understand me better. In his eyes, I am just a silly girl who just grew up. If he can enjoy my fresh body now, he will enjoy my warm heart someday. One day he will know that he has dramatically misjudged me. Thinking of this, I cannot help but smile. Jack, who has just rested, notices my smile.

"What's going on in your little head?" he asks.

"Something more than you can imagine," I reply.

Jack's mouth curls into a small smile, which he usually wears when mocking people.

"How do you feel? Satisfied?"

I don't want to reply.

"Want another one?" His mocking eyes have turned into a smirk. "You greedy little night-grazing filly." As he speaks, his hands start to move on me again.

No. Jack is wrong. I'm not a filly. I'm not a loose woman either. It's my lack of wisdom to let Jack judge me so wrongly. It must be fixed, and I must fix it now.

I move Jack's hands away calmly. Jack looks at me curiously, expecting my further reactions. Suddenly I jump up from the grass and walk to the bench.

"Jack, I love you far more than I love myself, but it doesn't mean you can do whatever you want with me."

"Come back, you little troublemaker," Jack yells at me, bowing his upper body.

I ignore him and quickly put on my evening dress.

Jack stays put on the grass, looks at me, and yells angrily, "Damn, what are you doing? Take those clothes off. Don't make me wait too long."

I straighten my messed-up hair and say to the self-righteous man in a calm tone, "Jack, I am Olivia, not 'Filly.' You are the first male to touch my body, and I hope you will be the last one." Then, I leave.

I leave Jack there alone.

Leaving Jack in the heat alone on the grass. . . I must be the first person on the set to do that. Jack doesn't need to attract others. As a billionaire, Jack has no shortage of women wherever he goes in Hollywood.

But I am different, I don't want Jack's money. I want his love.

A few days later, I enter the studio, ready for another day of rehearsals. As soon as I step inside, I see Jack.

He is walking out of the building with one of the key people in our studio. Jack strides out, and each step announces his confidence. We are face-to-face and less than a few feet apart. There is no way he cannot see me. He's acting like I don't even exist. Until Jack passes by, he doesn't even look in my direction, his eyes fixed on the person next to him.

I feel a pang of pain in my chest. I know Jack must still be angry with me.

We cross paths again in the dining hall during lunch break. I switch to another line to avoid him. Later, I pick a table in the corner. Even though I still catch his eye, I can't help but look at him. He's so handsome, his dark hair falling over his forehead, his blue eyes piercing and intense. He is still one of the most eye-catching men around. But there's a hardness to him now, a wall that he's built up around himself.

When he puts on a straight face, gulps down food, and ignores everything around him, I'm the only one who knows why. In the middle of the night, the proud and invincible Prince Charming Jack was abandoned on the green grass by someone he didn't care about. It must be uncomfortable, especially when he was in such high spirits. I don't blame him. Turning a domineering boss into an angry doormat was an extraordinary act of mine. I smile in silence.

I hide half my face behind a burger and watch him quietly. I can feel his eyes on me, watching me closely.

Jack is doing the same thing and is still interested in me.

I wish we could talk to clear the air between us. But I know he needs to be ready for that. When I walk out of the dining hall, I bring back my confidence. I return to my work in a better mood. I'm winning.

I like the fresh air. I take the script, walk to the water fountain, and sit under the tree. I study the new script, my heart racing with excitement. This is it, the big break for which I've been waiting. I'm the lead actress in this romantic movie.

I scan the pages, soaking in the plot and the characters. My role is an agent who poses as a singer to gain the trust of German officers and help rescue American prisoners of war. As they work together, the agent and her partner fall in love, but their dangerous mission puts them both at risk. It's a story that's been told many times before, but I know I can bring something new to the role.

As I work on my lines and character, I get lost in the story. Jack, the guy who was offended by me, returned to me. The male protagonist in the script is resolute, intelligent, and domineering, and his words and deeds are too like Jack's. Whenever I see his lines, I can hear Jack's voice, I can see Jack's actions, and I can even feel Jack's hands on me.

Moreover, the heroine in this script is simply a replica of me, and I can play her perfectly if I rely on my true colors. I know the omnipotent Jack can write a movie script in a few days.

Is this Jack's masterpiece?

When I put all the puzzle pieces together, I see a pair of solid hands in the background, working everything silently.

From rushing to write the script to setting up the photography team, from auditioning to recruiting actors, until I finally became the leading actress. Yes, I got this position through competition. Still, the lead role in this script is tailor-made for me.

Oh, Jack, only Jack could do this. But he never leaked a word to me. His voice was cold even when he told me about the audition schedule.

But why?

Why did Jack do all this?

Is this his way of apologizing to me?

I don't know.

If I have an opportunity to talk to him again, I'll ask these questions, and I'll owe him thanks.

I put the script down on the bench and ask myself, *should I talk to him first if I meet Jack again in public?*

The answer is a big NO.

What if I meet him in private?

The answer is still a big NO.

Jack is an intelligent man. After I told him he was my first man and wished he could be my last man, he should clearly understand he is the only one I love. If he chooses to avoid me, I should see it as a rejection.

If Jack rejects my love, then I should not beg for his.

It's sad. But it's my choice.

I keep my feelings to myself; I devote myself wholeheartedly to the preparatory work of the film. Every line, every look, every movement, I have been carefully rehearsing repeatedly.

One day, when I'm rehearsing a particularly emotional scene, with tears on my face, Jack shows up on set.

Should I continue my practice?

Then I notice Jack walking towards me, and I freeze. I stare at him, my heart racing in my chest.

My big NO has disappeared.

"Hey," he says, his voice low and hesitant.

"Hi," I reply, trying to keep my voice steady. I do not want my coworkers to notice the secret between Jack and me.

"I heard you are doing very well," he says, looking at me with those piercing blue eyes.

"Thank you," I say politely, feeling a flush rise to my cheeks.

"That's amazing," he says, his eyes lighting up. "Can I watch you rehearse?"

I nod, feeling a mix of excitement and nervousness.

After I complete my performance, we watch the rest of the rehearsal together. Jack picks a seat near me. I can feel the warmth of his body, the scent of his cologne.

And I know that I'm in trouble.

Jack sends me a text message saying he wants me to wait until after the rehearsal is over.

The time becomes slow. I can't wait to spend time with Jack.

When the rehearsal is finally over, after everyone leaves, we sit on a bench together watching the sunset. The air is cool and crisp, but I don't feel the chill.

"I've been thinking a lot about you," he says suddenly, his voice low and intense.

"Me too." I sigh. "Hey, Jack," I say, my heart racing. "Did you write the script yourself?"

"Yes, it was me," he replies with a smile.

I can only say two words. "Thank you!"

Jack looks at me. His expression is serious. "There's something I need to tell you."

"What is it?" I ask, feeling a sense of unease.

"I wanted to protect you and ensure you started on the right foot." Jack's voice is deep.

So, *Jack was protecting me* when he removed me from the earlier film and created a new script for me.

I feel a mix of emotions—grateful that he was looking out for me but hurt that he didn't trust me to make my own decisions.

"But I can handle any role," I protest.

"No one can," he says, taking my hand. "We all have limits."

I understand where he's coming from, and I can't help but feel touched by his concern.

"Thank you for looking out for me," I say, turning to look at him. "Why did you?" I ask. I know the answer I want to hear.

Jack does not answer. Instead, he takes my hand in his. We sit silently for a moment, just enjoying each other's company.

And then he leans in, his lips meeting mine in a soft, gentle kiss.

This kiss sends shivers down my spine, making me forget about everything else.

This is a gentle kiss, not a wild bite.

It is the first time he has treated me with respect.

It is the first time he's touched me like a gentleman to a lady, not a monster to a victim.

"I think I may love you," he whispers, his eyes fixed on mine.

Jack loves me! I know it. Even he says he thinks he may.

These are the words I have wanted to hear since I was a little girl.

I don't know how many times I quietly hid outside my brother's bedroom door, secretly listening to Jack's voice; I don't know how many times I silently watched him disappear at the end of the street with my brother. I really wanted to catch up with them. Still, I was worried about revealing my little secret. I don't know how many times I wished I would grow up soon enough to have the courage to tell him I've had a crush on him for years....

"Forgive me, will you?" Jack's voice is deep and gentle.

"Love doesn't need forgiveness," I reply, tears filling my eyes.

Jack replies with a long, warm, breathless kiss. It's a kiss I will remember for life.

We sit there and watch the beautiful sunset. Gold, pink, purple, and other brilliant colors blend like the light of happiness in our hearts.

"I love you," he says again.

"Do you?" I question, looking into his eyes.

Jack looks at me seriously, as if he has made a critical decision and is about to sign an important agreement. "I believe so." His voice is filled with emotion. "I've never said l-o-v-e to anyone."

I'll remember this moment no matter what happens next.

Chapter 6. Jack

I never thought I could fall in love with anyone. But now I've broken my own rule.

Since I told Olivia I loved her that evening, two weeks have passed. Now, it's the end of May. I'm in the woods, standing inside the tent, watching the shoot.

It's Olivia's first feature film. Nothing can go wrong. I put one of the best directors, James, in charge of the filming.

The filmed scene depicts Olivia as the undercover agent with the singer's identity, on a stormy day, waiting for her boyfriend to join her and run away.

The rain is hard. The branches wave heavily in the wind.

Good. The film needs real thunder and lightning.

The crew is ready, and all the cameras are well-covered. This equipment is expensive.

Olivia is in front of the camera, exposed to the storm. I notice that her eyes are half-closed.

"Can you please open your eyes? We need to get this shot right," James instructs. Olivia nods. She stands there, shivering, and wet, waiting for the director to say "cut."

"Cut! That was great, Olivia!" the director roars.

Olivia runs back to the tent. Her whole costume is soaked.

I shake my head. "No, it's not. Her expression isn't right. We need to do it again."

Olivia looks at me with a pleading expression. "Can't we do it tomorrow? I'm cold."

"No, we need to get it done today," I say firmly. "We have a tight schedule and can't afford to waste any time."

Olivia sighs and walks back into the rain. She stands there, waiting for the director to yell "action."

"Action!" the director yells.

Olivia stands in the rain, her hair sticking to her face and her clothes drenched. She looks sad and scared, precisely as her character should be.

"Cut! That was perfect!" James yells.

Olivia runs back to the tent and grabs a hot coffee. The water rolls down from her hair.

I'm not happy with the director.

"No, it's not perfect. Redo it. I don't see an expression of hope on her face."

The director does not dare argue with me. With a gesture, Olivia goes back to the storm.

We redo the shot at least fifteen times. Finally, I say, "Cut." Then we're done with this scene. I nod my head in approval. "Finally, we got it. Let's move on to the next scene."

The crew packs up their equipment, and we move on to the following location. I can't help but feel a sense of satisfaction. It's not easy being a movie producer, but when everything goes right, it's worth it.

As we set up for the next scene, I notice Olivia sitting alone on a nearby log. She's still wet from the rain, and her face looks tired.

"Are you okay, Olivia?" I ask, walking over to her.

"I'm fine," she says, forcing a smile.

"You did a great job today," I say, trying to be friendly.

Olivia looks at me, her expression changing. She says, "You know, it's not easy being an actress. We must do things we don't want to, like standing in the rain for hours. And all for what? A movie?"

I nod my head, understanding. "I know it's not easy. But it's worth it. When the movie comes out, and people love it, it makes everything worth it."

Olivia nods, a small smile on her face. "Yeah, I guess you're right."

We continue shooting for the rest of the day, and everything goes smoothly. As we wrap up the day, I can't help but feel proud of what we've accomplished. Making a movie is demanding work, but it's magic when it all comes together.

"Great job today, everyone," I say, clapping my hands together. "Let's do it again tomorrow."

The crew packs up their equipment, and we return to our hotel.

As I lie in bed, I can't help but think about the movie we're making. It will be great, and I can't wait for people to see it. I close my eyes and drift off to sleep, dreaming about the next day of shooting.

The next day, we arrive on set early, ready to start. The sun is shining, and the woods are alive with birds singing.

"Morning, Boss," the director greets me as I step out of the car.

"Morning. Let's get to work," I reply, sipping my coffee.

Olivia walks over to us, looking bright-eyed and ready to go.

"Morning, Olivia," I tease her. "You ready for another day of standing in the rain?"

Olivia laughs. "I'll do whatever it takes to make this movie great."

We start setting up the first scene of the day. It's a chase scene where Olivia's character runs through the woods, trying to escape from her enemies.

"Okay, Olivia, we're going to need you to run through the woods and then hide behind that tree," James explains.

Olivia nods and takes her mark. "Got it."

"Action!" the director yells.

Olivia runs through the woods, her hair flying behind her. She looks back and sees the enemies getting closer. She ducks behind a tree, trying to catch her breath.

"Cut!" the director yells. "That was great, Olivia. Let's do it again, but can you look more scared this time?"

Olivia nods. "Got it."

"Action!" James yells.

Olivia runs through the woods again, this time looking more scared. She hides behind the tree, her breathing heavy.

"Cut! That was perfect," James says.

"No, redo it. Olivia needs to run her tail off when she runs for her life. Graceful is shit," I disagree with the director. "Don't lower the bar."

I watch Olivia run until exhausted, then say, "Cut." Exhausted is what it should be.

"Great job, Olivia. Let's move on to the next scene," James says.

I nod my head in approval.

We shoot scene after scene, each one better than the last. The sun is setting, and we're finishing up the final scene of the day.

The camera crew is ready. The cameras all aim at a large oak tree from different angles and heights.

"Okay, Olivia, in this scene, you're going to have to climb up that tree," the director explains.

Olivia looks at the tall tree, an expression of uncertainty on her face. "Jack, this isn't in the script."

"I just added it." My voice is firm.

"Is this necessary?" Olivia asks.

"Yes. After I saw this tree."

Olivia looks down at her skirt.

I know what she's thinking. Her skirt will be inconvenient when she climbs up, exposing her legs to the camera.

However, this is what the plot requires. A well-trained female agent would not struggle like Olivia does. Hiding in the dense tree canopy is the safest option when search parties comb through the forest. I know Olivia was a very skillful tree climber as a child. She could climb higher than her brother.

"You can do it, Olivia," I encourage her. "We're almost done for the day."

Olivia takes a deep breath and starts climbing the tree.

She makes it to the top, then hides.

"Cut!" the director yells. "That's a wrap for today!"

Olivia looks down at me with a smile on her face. She may remember the tree house we had when we were kids.

We all cheer, happy to be done for the day. Olivia climbs down from the tree, beaming with pride.

"You did it, Olivia!" I say, patting her on the back.

Olivia laughs. "I never thought I'd be able to climb a tree again in my life."

The crew packs up their equipment and we return to the hotel.

As the movie crew returns to the hotel, the production manager quickly orders food and drinks for everyone. I'm exhausted, but I know there's still work to do. I tell the director inside the elevator, "Make sure everyone gets their food. I need to make a touch-up on the script."

James nods.

When I say, "touch-up," Olivia glances at me like she wants to ask a question. Before she gets a chance, the elevator door opens, and we split to different floors.

I head to my room for a much-needed shower. As the hot water washes over me, my muscles relax. I recall how Olivia climbed the tree; I can't hold back my laugh. That was one of my creations on the shooting field. Then, I close my eyes and take a deep breath to clear my head and think of new modifications.

Just as I finish showering, I hear a knock at the door. I wrap a towel around myself and head to answer it, expecting to see the food delivery guy. I'm surprised to see Olivia standing there, looking anxious. She must have just gotten out of the shower too since her hair is still wet. She wears a loose white cotton shirt and looks comfortable.

"Hey, Olivia. What's up?" I ask, curious.

I look out at the hallway. I don't want any of the crew members to see this. Good, there's no one there. No matter how much I want to pick her up and drop her on my king-size bed, I'd prefer to meet her in the conference room instead. Never mix business with personal life. It's my rule.

"It's about the script," Olivia says, biting her lip nervously. "Jack, if you have any new modifications, I want to be ready before tomorrow on the field."

"Olivia, we can discuss this with the director in the conference room or lobby." It will be an innovative idea to discuss with the director and the lead actress simultaneously. "Wait here," I say. I want to close the door and return inside, and I need to put on my clothes.

"I want to talk to you first. I need to understand what's behind all your modifications, so I can perform better," Olivia insists.

I turn and look into her eyes, her shining eyes. I nod my head, impressed by her dedication. "Come on in. Let's look."

Just as we sit down, there's a knock at the door. It's our food.

We eat while discussing the latest changes to the script. I relax a little, enjoying the rare downtime on this hectic shoot.

After dinner, we sit at the table, and I pull out my laptop.

Olivia leans in, her eyes focused on the screen.

"I've made a few changes to the dialogue in the next few scenes," I say, scrolling through the script. "I think it will make it more dramatic."

Olivia nods, her eyes scanning the page.

I stand behind her.

I can see she isn't wearing a bra. But why?

It's because she just got out of the shower and wanted to completely relax her body after working for more than ten hours.

God, she's come to seduce me on purpose.

From the open collar, without unbuttoning, I can see her breasts as round as balls. They are plump, soft, and more attractive than fresh peaches on the tree.

Whatever the reason, I can't resist the temptation under that shirt for another second. I know inside this loose shirt; my hands can move freely. Olivia is still reading the script. She has no clue about all the dirty thoughts in my mind. She also doesn't see the risk she faces by walking inside my room.

"Yeah, I like that. It'll give my character more depth," she says.

No reply from me. My eyes aren't focused on the screen.

She looks up at me, and her face suddenly turns shy and red. In the dim light, it makes her more beautiful. I hold my hands tightly together. I don't want to offend Olivia. Now I know this little kitty can turn into a female tiger in a second. When did I become afraid of this girl?

Then I see a miracle change in Olivia. She closes her eyes, picks up my hand, and puts her shy face on mine.

I stroke her still-damp hair with love in my heart, a feeling I've never felt before. It doesn't come from my senses driving me crazy, but from a deep compassion that makes me think unspeakable good. This is the first time I have felt this extraordinary artistic conception. The feeling is powerful, unlike when I first told Olivia I loved her that evening. This is the difference between like and love. I don't want to destroy this warm feeling.

For the next hour, my fingers are not inside her shirt but on the keyboard. My thoughts are laser-focused and aimed at the lines of the script. We go over it together, making minor tweaks here and there. We also discuss all related key performance actions. I see a different Olivia, a clever, talented, and lovely Olivia. I can tell that she's really invested in her character.

But just as we get into the groove, my phone starts ringing. I scowl at the screen, recognizing the caller's name: Emily.

"Ugh, what does she want now?" I mutter. I must answer her call since she's in the middle of filming and things are chaotic. I step away from the table.

"Hey," I say. I expect some complaints from her.

"Hey, Boss!" Emily's voice is syrupy and sweet, but I can detect a hint of smugness behind it. "Just wanted to check in and see how the shoot is going over there."

I roll my eyes. "Why do you ask?"

Emily laughs. "Boss, I was just wondering if there's any chance I could swing by and visit you guys on set. I miss you guys!"

I feel a pang of annoyance. "No. We're busy here," I say, rejecting her request firmly. The shooting field is not a shopping mall. I do not need a visitor. When Emily keeps asking, and I notice a coming call from Alex, the director, on the other line, I cut the call with Emily and pick up Alex's call. I realize something must have happened on the other end.

"Hey, Jack, we've got a problem on set."

I can tell Alex is in a bad mood. "What's going on?"

"Emily's been getting a little too 'friendly' with some crew members," Alex says. "I'm going to have to remove her from the production."

"Are you serious? She's the lead actress!" Their film has already completed 20% of shooting, which means financial losses.

Alex's voice is heavy as he says, "I know, but I can't risk any drama on set. We've got a tight schedule to keep. I can change the script and save the film."

"I understand," I say. It sometimes happens, no matter how excellent the plan was. A car accident, a pregnancy, or a troublemaker actress can lead to this situation. "Do you have a replacement in mind?"

Alex sighs deeply and his voice relaxes. "Thank you, Boss. Not yet, but I'm working on it. I'll let you know as soon as I find someone."

"Alright, keep me posted. This is not good news." I pick up the wine. I need something cold.

Alex's voice becomes cheerful, "I know, but it's better to deal with it now before it gets out of hand."

"I guess you're right. Find your replacement." I drink it all.

"I'm sure we will. We've got a talented team; we'll figure it out," Alex replies calmly.

Whenever I hear this calm tone, I know he must already have a plan in his mind.

I refill the glass of wine and sit back on the sofa. I need a little relaxation.

Olivia is sitting in front of the desk. She must sense something is going wrong.

"Jack, are you okay?" Her face is caring.

"Yapa. Piece of cake." I drop the glass on the end table.

"It seems the taste of the cake isn't very good," she says, seeing me drinking sullenly and starting to make fun of me.

How dare she? I stare at her.

"I can change the flavor for you." Olivia's face suddenly flushes. She gets up, walks to me, and sits on the sofa's armrest.

She's so close.

If I turned my head sideways, my teeth could bite her nipples, and I really want to bite harder this time. I have too many things building up inside of me.

"Presumptuous. Why did you come to see me dressed like this?" I asked angrily.

I can't stretch myself anymore.

Her soft voice melts my heart. "Jack, I wore this shirt for you. It's my pajamas for tonight. I want to give myself to you in love and thanks."

"Remember, I do not have any commitment to you. It doesn't matter if I love you or not," I repeat. No commitment. I must make it truly clear.

"I know."

She put her breasts against my face. I feel the warmth and softness again.

"The only commitment I need is from me in my heart," she says softly.

I turn out the light.

Chapter 7. Olivia

I awake from my sleep, dimly aware that I'm in Jack's bed, and sit up with a start.

The hotel is quiet. Jack is in a deep sleep with his hands spread out. Even in his sleep, this guy spreads his hands and feet as if he is the king of the world. I laugh silently in the dark.

I move slightly, slip off his bed, pick up my shoes, and walk out of Jack's room barefoot. I put on my shoes outside the door and leave. I don't want to be seen by anyone. My white top is full of wrinkles, which will give away my secrets without me saying a word.

I return to my room without incident. I'm fortunate that I do not meet anyone in the elevator. I just see a few people in the corridor, leaving with their suitcases.

I know I need a bath before going to work. When I lie down in the warm water, I keep thinking about Jack.

Jack is a guy who will try his best to get whatever he wants, and he does the same with sex. I can still feel Jack's imprint on my body. My breasts are swollen, slightly sore. They are the first to be heavily targeted each time before Jack launches his stormy all-out attack. I need to buy a new bra, because under Jack's hands, my breasts become much fuller than before.

While I'm thinking about Jack's strong hands, my cell phone starts vibrating. Jack's message appears on the screen.

Morning. That's short. It's Jack's style.

Good morning. I give back one more word, then I put down my phone.

The phone vibrates again. *How are you? I hope I didn't hurt you after drinking.*

I smile and reply, *No worries, I'm unscathed.*

Jack is a willful tyrant in bed, especially after drinking. After turning off the lights last night, he didn't say a tender word of love. What came out of his throat was a beast-like low growl. His hands were like iron claws, his powerful sucking accompanied by ruthless biting, and his muscular body was tireless.

I don't know if Jack will remember his drunken madness, but I will not leak a single word about what he did last night. I don't want him to have any constraints with me. Jack is a tough guy. With his status as a billionaire and superhuman wisdom, he overwhelms all obstacles in front of him. Still, I know he's under pressure that three heroes could not bear.

I only want him to be at ease when he is with me... because I love him. I love his boundless creativity and will that no one can conquer, and I love what he has done for me.

My cell phone rings. "Olivia, I'm sorry. I drank too much yesterday. I must have been rough—"

I cut him off. "Jack, I've grown up and love everything about you." His words touch me. Very few people worldwide could hear Jack say sorry.

Jack pauses. Then, switching to his usual businesslike tone, he says, "Get ready. Heading out in half an hour. Need to do early morning shots."

"Yes, Boss," I reply, also in a tone of dead seriousness. Jack bursts into a happy laugh on the other side of the phone.

Amidst his laughter, I hang up the phone and jump out of the tub.

I must dry my hair quickly.

Half an hour later, the crew sits in the big bus bound for the forest area.

After the bus leaves the asphalt, it drives onto a gravel road, followed by a dirt road. When facing the overgrown woods, it stops. The city is far away from here. We are in the wilderness.

I don't have many shots in the morning, so I'll have a satisfying meal. I end up eating enough for two because I shared Jack's dinner last night, which was not enough.

I hold a Coke in my left hand and pizza in my right hand. I eat three pieces of pizza in a row. The assistant removes the plate when I reach for the fourth piece.

"Oh, the boss said you have overeaten," the fat assistant says shyly.

I follow the gaze of the assistant and see Jack standing in the distance, staring at me angrily.

Well, that doesn't make sense. However, I can only give up resentfully.

Half an hour later, when I play the female agent running to escape from the jungle, I understand why Jack was angry. I overate, my stomach is heavy, and running becomes uncomfortable. How silly I was. Jack might think I am a stupid food lover. I feel embarrassed.

Jack seems to want to punish me for overeating too much. He makes me jump on the grass repeatedly.

I feel the grass beneath my feet and the sun beating down on my skin. I'm dazzled and dizzy.

I slow down.

"Keep jumping," Jack barks, pointing a finger in my direction. His tone is harsh, as if I've committed some great offense. Many team members are watching.

I realize that I'm not going to be granted any rest by bossy Jack.

With a deep sigh, I resume my jumping.

Up and down, up and down, I bounce on the grass.

I feel my head spinning and my vision blurring, but I can't stop. I'm trapped in grumpy Jack's grip, and he's determined to make me suffer.

Jack watches me from distance, his arms crossed—what a bossy man!

"Get the camera crew ready," Jack barks to the director.

"Camera!" James yells.

I finally get a chance to take a break when the crew starts setting up the cameras. Unexpectedly, just as I stop, Jack points at me and shouts, "Keep jumping."

His voice is fierce as if I'm his enemy for three generations.

In full view of the crew, I'm embarrassed. I've got no choice but to keep jumping.

When I'm about to collapse from exhaustion, I hear Jack tell the director, "Start shooting."

"Camera crew, get ready," James yells loudly.

"Action!"

On James's order, I follow the pre-set route, running high and low in the wild grass. I don't need to act. I've already entered a state of exhaustion.

"Cut."

When I return to the original place, I see Jack talking to James and pointing to the stream not far away. This doesn't look good. I know Jack has a new idea. He just worked out his newly revised script last night, and now he'll make some more revisions on the spot.

Sure enough, James comes to me, points to the stream, and says, "Olivia, we need more footage on the escape. You'll have to cross the field first, then wade through the stream and hide in the opposite woods...."

I glance at Jack, who is explaining to the camera crew and ignores me. "Oh, Jack, my love," I sigh silently.

Then I notice a white jeep pulling up nearby. I squint my eyes to get a better look and realize that it's Emily. My heart sinks as I remember her sneaky behavior and selfish attitude from the last time we worked together.

"What is she doing here?" I mutter under my breath, hoping that she's not going to cause any trouble.

Emily strides over to us, looking stunning in a sleek black dress and high heels. She greets the director with a hug and then moves on to Jack. However, Jack gives her a rude "stop" gesture, clearly not interested in giving her a warm welcome.

Emily looks embarrassed for a moment before taking a seat on a nearby folding chair.

"Hi, everyone. I finally found you here," she says, trying to sound casual. "How nice to be in the woods." She smiles sweetly.

"What do you want, Emily?" Jack asks, his voice dripping with disdain.

Emily clears her throat, looking uncomfortable. "Well, I heard about this project, and I wanted to see if there was a role for me. I know what happened last time wasn't ideal, but I promise I've learned from my mistakes."

I roll my eyes, not buying her excuse for a second.

Jack doesn't look convinced either. "We've already cast all the roles, Emily. Sorry." Then Jack turns to the director. "Let's start."

"Is the camera crew ready?" James asks.

"Yep," replies the person in charge of the photography team.

The director turns to me. "Olivia, are you ready?"

"Yes," I say.

James lifts both arms, gestures to the camera crew and leads sound control, then drops his arm. "Action."

As I begin to run through the wild grass, I can feel the blades brushing against my skin, leaving small scratches and cuts. The sun beats down on my back, and I can feel the sweat pouring down my face.

The grass is tall and wild, reaching up to my waist. It's a beautiful shade of green, but I don't have time to appreciate it. Even if there is a snake here, I will keep running.

I just keep running, my feet pounding against the ground.

As I approach the stream, I can see the muddy ground looming in front of me. The soil beneath my feet becomes soft and squishy, and I can feel my shoes sinking into the mud. It's a struggle to keep running, and I can feel my muscles burning with exhaustion.

But I don't give up. I keep pushing forward, my feet sinking deeper and deeper into the mud. I can feel the muck clinging to my shoes, making it difficult to move.

Finally, I reach the stream, the water rushing over my feet. It's wide and shallow, and I can see rocks jutting out from the water. I take a deep breath and prepare to keep going.

But then I hear the director's voice booming behind me. "Stop!"

I stand there and wait. "What's going on?" I ask.

"Olivia, come back, do it again," James yells through the horn.

When I return to the original location, I find out that someone made a slight sound during the filming, by accident. The sound control person caught it so the shot must be done again.

So, I start my second escape.

This time, I'm less lucky than the first time. I run on the grass with mud-filled shoes, my feet slip, and I fall.

So, I start my third run.

I take a deep breath. I know that I need to make it count. My heart is racing as I run through the grass, the wind whipping past me.

Finally, I reach the stream, and I can see the rocks jutting out from the water. I try to be careful, but the rocks are slippery, and I lose my footing. I fall hard, the water rushing over me and soaking my clothes.

I groan in pain, feeling my knees throbbing with agony. I try to stand, but I stumble, my legs shaking with exhaustion. I run to the opposite bank and hide behind a big tree, my heart pounding in my chest.

"Cut." I hear the pleasant voice from James.

I'm relieved and grateful that the scene is over. I stumble back to the director, feeling embarrassed and ashamed. But then I see both James and Jack smiling at me, and I feel a surge of hope.

"Great job," Jack says, his voice full of admiration. "You really nailed it this time."

James looks at my bleeding knee and shakes his head. "That looks very real," he says, his voice full of concern. "Let's get that cleaned up."

My assistant rushes over to help me, cleaning my wound and bandaging it up. I feel grateful for their kindness, even though I'm still in pain.

But then the sound control team leader comes over, looking serious. "Boss, we have to do it again," he says, his face grim.

I feel my heart sink as I realize that something has gone wrong.

"What happened?" I ask, my voice shaking.

"It seems that someone coughed quietly when you were hiding behind the tree," the team leader explains. "It sounded like a woman's voice."

I look at my bleeding leg and realize that the scene has been ruined. The feeling is more painful than my leg.

Jack turns to Emily, He's angry. "Did you cough?" he demands.

Emily looks surprised, her eyes wide with innocence. "No, it wasn't me," she says, trying to sound convincing.

Jack doesn't believe her for a second. "Get out of here," he snarls. "You're not welcome here."

Emily walks away, looking dejected and humiliated.

From Jack's angry tone, I know why Emily stopped by.

She was here to make trouble. She wanted to take the heroine's position from me again. But Jack protected me.

He looks at me apologetically and asks, "Can you do it again?"

I smile and say with a firm tone, "No problem."

This time, the take goes smoothly.

As the sun begins to dip below the horizon, the sky is painted with shades of pink and orange. The trees surrounding the set cast long shadows and the air is crisp.

We are waiting for dark; there are still a few night scenes left to shoot. Some team members retreat to the RV for a rest, while others gather around a crackling campfire.

I'm exhausted after a long day of shooting, and I crave some peace and quiet. I walk to the edge of the woods, seeking solace in the serene surroundings. I lean against a sturdy tree, gazing up at the stars twinkling in the night sky.

I see Jack sitting by the campfire, chatting with the directors and team leaders. His mind is always active, even in the field, and he's constantly thinking of innovative ideas and ways to improve the shot.

As I stand there, I can hear the murmur of their voices in the distance, and the occasional burst of laughter. But mostly, it's quiet and peaceful, with only the sound of the wind rustling through the leaves and the distant call of a nocturnal animal.

I take a deep breath, feeling the cool night air fill my lungs. Then, I hear the snapping of branches. Someone is coming over.

Who is this person?

I start looking around, but I can only hear footsteps occasionally. Someone is playing hide-and-seek with me, dodging very quickly, obviously exceptionally good at this.

Suddenly, I'm hugged from behind. From the familiar smell of cologne, I know it is Jack.

"It's too risky," I say, starting to get nervous. "I don't want to be seen."

Jack stops me from talking by kissing me.

He says gravely, "I know I was hard on you."

I reply equally gravely, "You are training me seriously."

Jack smiles and asks, "Do you know why I keep revising the script?"

I also smile and reply, "Because art has no limits."

Jack sighs. "You're a good girl."

I ask, "Is that all?"

"Don't be too greedy," Jack teases a little impatiently.

"It's too late." I stare at Jack. "You can't do without me." My voice is firm.

Jack stares into my eyes. He is silent for a while. And then he mutters, "Really? Will I really be unable to leave you?"

Chapter 8. Jack

The big bus runs on a two-way road in the suburbs. On both sides of the road is dense woodland. It's dark ahead, and we can only see limited scenery in the bus's headlights, including occasional deer dazed by the light at the edge of the forest.

It's already four o'clock in the morning. The big bus is quiet, and most people have fallen asleep from exhaustion. I glance back and find Olivia leaning against the bus window in a dream. The smile on her lips makes her look a little more childish and naughtier than when she is working.

"It's too late," her words ring in my ears again. *"You can't do without me."* I shake my head and smile in the dark. *Really? Am I inseparable from this little girl?*

After returning to the hotel, I only rest for two hours. I wake up to the sound of my phone buzzing incessantly. I get up and return to work. During the two days of staying in the woods, I got a lot of work done there.

I lean against the headboard and start checking my phone. The first thing I see are emails from the director of my latest movie, *Alien Invasion*. I watch a few new film samples from him.

Great! The background of the film is very novel and creative. But why do I not feel excited?

I watch it again, then figure it out.

The battle between humans and aliens needs to be more spectacular. It needs more sound and more lights.

I quickly scroll through and reply: *Looks good. Add more explosions and flash charges. Hurry up!*

I check my schedule, and next up, I need to finalize the cast for my upcoming romantic comedy.

I quickly review the case name list and call my assistant, Jay.

"Good morning, Jack." Jay's voice is always so polite.

"Let Peter play the male lead. Emily, the female lead, needs to be replaced." As I say that, I look at the list of names and start screening the actresses in my mind.

"Daniel, the director, has initially selected Emily." Jay's voice sounds a little hesitant.

Here's Emily again. This young lady must be busier than me recently. She must have played tricks on the director behind my back. I can't give Emily another chance to mess with my projects.

I bark at my assistant, "Get me Daniel on the line now!" I need to make this a three-line conversation.

Soon, I hear the director's voice. "Good morning, Jack."

I get straight to the point: "Daniel, I need you to change the lead actress in my new comedy movie. Get Scarlett Johansson. Yes, or no?"

"Jack, do we have to change the lead? Emily is a good fit," he says, but from his voice I can tell he's hiding something.

"Emily is a good fit for a public relationship," I say, raising my voice. "I don't care what kind of deals you've made with Emily. You'll have to pay her back from your pockets if you owe her anything. I won't give this snake a second chance to mess with me. Remember, she will have zero chances from me."

After a brief hesitation, Daniel agrees. "Yes, Boss. But can you tell me why?"

"All I can say to you is this call will save you a lot of trouble. Jay, can you notify the operations manager about the lead change?"

"Sure." Jay sounds relieved.

"Great, bye!" I hang up and check the time. I have ten minutes before the Zoom meeting.

I walk into the bathroom for a quick shower. When I put on my shirt, I'm running two minutes late for my Zoom meeting with the studio executives. I have no time to put on my pants.

I sit in front of my screen, and I'm greeted by a screen full of suits.

One of my old buddies' jokes about my wet messy hair. "Wow, Jack, your hair looks great."

Then, I heard a burst of laughter. "Jack, are you just getting out of the swimming pool?"

I must look a little embarrassed. But I have no time for this. Every one of the attendants is creative, with super imagination. They can pop a comedy scene here.

"What's the holdup?" I demand. Everyone stops laughing and shifts into work mode. "We need to greenlight my new action thriller now!"

One of the executives looks hesitant. "We're not sure the budget can handle it." Another one supports the executive's opinion.

I know all the numbers, and they are looking for an excuse for the mismanagement of their budget. I don't have time for their excuses. "I'll assign a manager to take over budget control today. So, it shouldn't be a problem," I say. I think I may have to fire that executive. He overspends on unnecessary things, including paying for a luxury hotel and high-end restaurant meals.

After I make up my mind, I say, "Listen up, we're making this movie, and we're making it big. Got it?"

After some heated back-and-forth, we finally reach an agreement.

The Zoom meeting is over. I'm glad I didn't forget to click "Leave" on the screen before standing up. I smirk. If these troublemakers had seen that I wasn't wearing pants, I'd be the butt of their jokes.

Then I receive a call from James. "Boss, we're about to leave in five minutes."

"Coming." I put on my jeans and head to the parking lot.

All the actors and actresses have already completed their makeup and are dressed like the French of the 1940s with a few German soldiers and officers.

I finish my breakfast on the moving bus.

Today we're shooting a crucial scene for our upcoming film. The team members have already blocked off an entire street in downtown LA, and we're ready to roll. Olivia is playing an American spy meeting her boyfriend, a German officer, in a coffee shop.

I like the street view. The coffee shop is tucked away on a quiet street, and the warm glow of the lights spills out onto the sidewalk, inviting passersby to come inside. We've got cameras set up inside and outside the shop, and the crew is excitedly buzzing.

I also like the inside of the coffee shop. It's cozy and neat, and the air is filled with the rich aroma of freshly brewed coffee and baked goods, creating a comforting and inviting atmosphere. The space is small, with only a handful of tables and chairs, but it's filled with character and charm.

Shelves of books and jars of homemade jams and preserves line the walls giving it a homey and rustic feel. The mismatched furniture with vintage armchairs and sofas is placed around wooden tables. It is the perfect spot to cozy up with an enjoyable book or catch up with friends.

James is super. He gets everything ready without wasting minutes. He barks orders at the cameramen and the extras, ensuring everyone is in their place and ready to go.

Then, "Action!" he shouts, and the scene begins.

The German officer and the spy sit across from each other, sipping coffee and exchanging whispers. The soft sound of 1940s music creates an atmosphere of a bygone age.

"Cut." The director drops his hand and goes to check the shot.

I lean against the wall and watch Olivia sitting in the chair, watching James. She must want to know how the take turns out.

I see the director shake his head. It hasn't passed.

Olivia stands up. "What's wrong?"

"You're supposed to love this officer. I can't see an expression of love. Try again."

"Sure." Olivia goes back to her chair.

"Action," the director says as he drops his hand.

James is right. I watch Olivia's performance closely. She smiles adorably, but it's a smile you would offer to friends or coworkers, not to a lover.

"Stop." The director must find the same thing. He walks over to Olivia. "Olivia, have you ever fallen in love with anyone?"

Olivia's face turns red. I hope she won't mention my name. But she doesn't even look at me.

She asks quietly, "How can I do better?"

James points at the German officer, saying, "Forget about his face. Think about the man you love sitting there. Can you do that?"

"Yes, I can try."

James goes back to the doorway. "Action," he yells again.

Olivia's face lights up under the camera with a radiant smile that seems to glow from within. Her eyes sparkle with joy and excitement, and her cheeks flush with a rosy hue.

I see signs of nervousness or shyness; she fidgets with her hands. Her body tends to lean toward the officer.

How familiar it is! It's what I see when she spends time with me. My heart is touched.

"Cut!" The director turns to the camera lead. "Did you get it?"

"Yes. It's good."

"Great. Let's move to the next scene." James smiles at me happily. "Olivia is good."

In the next scene, the spy and officer leave the coffee shop. German undercover agents follow the spy.

I look at the street view. I must agree the crew picked the right set.

It's remarkably like the scenery in 1940s France; the street is alive with activity. Tall trees and colorful flowers dot the sidewalks, making it a picturesque sight. Colorful buildings with unique architecture and charm line the streets.

Horse-drawn carriages echo through the alleys along the cobblestone streets. The buildings have intricate balconies and wrought-iron railings. The ornate details are a testament to the city's rich history and culture. In the distance, the spire of a towering church reaches to the heavens.

The men dress in tailored suits and women in elegant dresses of the period. It's a time of sophistication and refinement, where beauty and art are highly valued.

We've created a powerfully emotional scene. Despite the looming threat of war, there's a sense of optimism. The street is alive with energy and creativity, and the people are determined to enjoy every moment of their lives.

As a movie producer, I'm grateful for the opportunity to capture its essence in film.

Then, a loud voice interrupts my thoughts.

"Cameras and start rolling," the director yells.

I watch them move like the army on the battlefield. This is an excellent team led by a strong leader—the director, James.

I love the idea of shooting a movie from a higher location and capturing the bustling activity of the street below.

I look at the director. "We need a vantage point high enough to capture a bird's-eye view of the street, but not so high that we lose the sense of intimacy and detail."

"Got it. We already found the perfect location last week. We'll use cranes, drones, and other specialized equipment to capture sweeping shots of the street below, and close-ups of the people and activity."

"Great." James is a man whose word I can count on.

I look at the church at the end of the street. "We need multiple cameras here to capture different angles and perspectives," I suggest.

"Right, it will give us a wide range of footage to work with in post-production," the director agrees. Then he passes the message to the camera lead. "Camera," the director yells with both hands raised.

"Ready."

"Okay."

The answers are from separate locations, and two men are already on the cranes.

"Actors."

"Ready," voices around us say.

"Action."

Olivia, the "spy," leaves the coffee shop alone. She takes a leisurely stroll down the street, enjoying the beautiful scenery.

We've got the cameras rolling, capturing every step and expression on her face.

But then, as she nears the church, she realizes two men are following her. Her senses are on high alert, and she tries to lose her pursuers. But they're persistent, and she starts to panic. Her boyfriend arrives to save the day just as she is about to be caught. He fights off the attackers, and they both make their escape.

We shoot the scene multiple times, tweaking the camera angles and lighting to get the perfect shot. It's a critical moment in the film, and we want to ensure we get it right.

I notice the kiss the "spy" gives to the "German officer" inside the church. It is a long kiss, and the emotion is so real. It makes the director happy.

"Good shot, good shot," James repeats to me.

I feel a little uncomfortable. I do not remember having this kind of feeling before.

When Olivia sits down to rest, I bring her a water bottle. She takes it, then gives it back to me. "I'm thirsty, but I can wait until I finish the next scene. I don't want to damage the makeup."

"Not a big deal, they can redo it, easy." I hand the water to her again.

She drinks very carefully and tries not to touch her lips.

I ask, "Do you like the German officer actor?"

"He's good," Olivia says, nodding.

"Do you love him?" I'm asking a stupid question.

"Yes." Olivia gives me a firm answer.

I feel surprised. How can Olivia care for someone so quickly?

She must sense my feelings.

"I love him in this movie. Did I do anything wrong?" Then she looks at me with a naughty smile.

I feel my face burning.

"You have really improved so much. You learned to be jealous." She jumps up from the chair and leans her head to her shoulder, laughing at me.

Behind her, many morning glories are hanging from the windowsill. She looks so cute. I really want to hug her. But I can't do it in front of these many eyes and cameras.

"Guys, get ready," the director calls. "We need to move to the next scene."

Olivia heads for the director. When she passes me, she tells me softly, "I kissed him with closed eyes, imagining I was kissing you."

I know what I want to say, but I can't say it in the daylight.

Olivia waves her hands and walks to the director cheerfully.

At this moment, I receive a text message reminding me I'm to attend a board meeting tomorrow. I know that I need to head back to the studio now, I need to complete my proposal for tomorrow's meeting.

"Olivia," I call. She stops, turns to me, and gives me a lovely smile. "Yes, Boss."

"I'm about to leave. I know you'll be fine." Before I finish my words, I see her smile is gone.

"When will you come back?" Olivia asks and moves a few steps toward me, but she stops. There are people around us.

"Olivia, I'm counting on you," I encourage her. "You'll be an excellent actress."

Olivia smiles softly, then turns and leaves. I can tell she doesn't want me to leave. I do not want to leave her either.

I watch Olivia walk away and realize how much I love her. Should I break my rule?

Chapter 9. Olivia

I haven't seen Jack since he returned to the studio. It has been a week. Since he left, I started feeling sick. I miss him so much.

Now, I stand in a space crowded with crew and equipment. The film set is in a hotel room and it's not easy to shoot within such a small area.

In this scene, the spy hides two of her team members in her room. Later, when the German soldiers arrive and search the hotel, there will be a fierce battle through hotel rooms and corridors, including fistfights and shootouts.

My heart races as I wait for the director to call "Action." I take a deep breath, trying to calm my nerves. I must pull my thoughts from Jack to the spy—my role. But my body feels different, my stomach a little queasy.

"Action," the director orders.

The scene begins.

When I try to focus on my lines and my co-star's performance, I feel a wave of nausea and struggle to keep it at bay. What is wrong with me?

As I walk off set, my costar looks at me with concern. "Are you okay?" he asks.

"I'm fine." I force a smile and nod, trying to pretend everything is all right. But deep down, I know something is wrong.

I stand in the doorway while the director checks on the shots. I can't stop thinking.

One question makes me incredibly nervous. What if I'm pregnant? The thought is thrilling and terrifying. I know that I'm not supposed to get pregnant right now.

When we have a ten-minute break, I walk to the restroom. On my way, every step feels like I'm walking toward a judge.

I take a deep breath and grab a pregnancy test from my bag. I bought this test during our lunch break. As I wait for the results, everything around me blurs, as if the universe is waiting anxiously with me. I close my eyes.

I hold my breath as I open my eyes. The test stick falls to the floor. It reads positive. I'm pregnant.

I'm scared.

However, after the initial fear disappears, a more pleasant feeling fills my heart.

The world in front of me is different now.

Even the oil paint on the wall seems to come to life. The colors, more vibrant and alive, take on new meaning, symbolizing hope, and renewal.

I'm creating a new life!

What a wonderful thing it would be to accompany a little one as he experiences countless firsts in his life! I will raise his little hand and let him comb the wind with his fingers for the first time, I will look at the sunrise and hear him say good morning for the first time, and I will watch him pick the crystal dewdrops on the green grass for the first time. I will learn to be a mother in the care of this little life, which will make my own life fuller. But along with the excitement comes fear and uncertainty. I start feeling tension. More questions are coming to my mind.

What will this mean for my career?

Will I be able to balance motherhood with my job?

Should I tell Jack about my pregnancy?

How will Jack deal with my pregnancy?

Will he interrupt our relationship with each other because of this?

After the ten-minute break, I walk back into the hotel room, the film set, waiting for the next shot. In this scene, I, "the spy," fight with a German soldier inside the room and the hallway.

I take a deep breath, trying to compose myself. I tell myself: I need to cheer up, and not let this pregnancy affect my performance on set.

"Action!" James yells. His voice is much louder inside the room than on the street.

I take a deep breath, steeling myself for the fight scene. The scenery around me, the elegant decor, and the plush furniture contrast with the scene's violence.

The room's door bursts open. The German soldier lunges towards me, and I kick him in the stomach. The scenery around me blurs as I focus on the fight, each move calculated and precise. Every action is well-designed by James.

We fight down the hallway, my kicks and punches landing with precision. With a final bang, the soldier goes down. Broken China falls onto the red carpet.

I hear James's yell, "Cut." I'm exhausted and relieved, as if the world's weight has been lifted from my shoulders.

"Olivia, we have to redo it." James walks over to me. "A spy should fight like a hitman. You ought to strike faster and harder." His face is unhappy.

Then, we do a second take. Unfortunately, I fail again. I throw a weak punch at the soldier, and I know why. I do not want to hurt my baby.

James approaches me, his tone stern. "What was that? You're supposed to be fighting for your life out there. You can't just freeze up like that." His voice is cold.

I take a deep breath, trying to hold back my tears. All I can say is, "I'm sorry."

Everyone, including the table and chairs around me, seem to mock my fears. It's as if the universe is against me.

The director sighs, his disappointment palpable. "Look, I understand that you may be ill. But you signed on for this movie, and we need you to give us your best."

I'm letting down everyone on set. Guilt is one of the worst feelings.

"Sorry, I'll try harder. I promise," I say.

James nods, but I can tell he's still disappointed.

The third time when the fight has just started in the hotel room, the director calls, "Stop." This time his voice is furious.

"Olivia," James says, his tone impatient. "We need to redo that fight scene again. You can't just freeze up like that." I take a deep breath and my nerves fray. James sighs. He stares at me. "We can't keep redoing this scene. You need to give it your all."

I nod, trying to hold back my tears.

I try again, but my kicks are weak, and my punches lack force. Before I take action, I hear a warning in my head each time: Olivia, you are a going to be a mom. Don't do anything to hurt your baby.

James calls, "Cut," and then he looks at me. "What's going on? You're not even trying," he snaps.

"I'm sorry, I just can't do this," I whisper.

James takes a deep breath, and his frustration is apparent. "This is tough, but we need you to give us your best. We're running out of time."

I gather my strength and try again. This time it barely passable, but it's not a good shot. I feel sad and guilty.

At night, on the way back to the hotel, I'm filled with fear, excitement, and uncertainty all rolled into one.

The lobby is bustling with people. When I pass by them, I feel lonely. I feel relief entering my room. The room is spacious and comfortable, and the wall decorations and light fixtures are elegant and tasteful. But very soon, despite the luxurious surroundings, I still can't find peace. This accidental pregnancy can change my life completely. I worry about my future and the impact this will have on my career and my relationship with Jack. He's always been clear about his rules: no family, no children. But now, with a baby on the way, I'm unsure what to do.

As I sit by the window gazing out, I'm greeted by a breathtakingly beautiful street night view that takes my breath away. The cityscape sprawls out before me, glittering like a sea of stars in the darkness, and the lights that twinkle in the distance create a magical atmosphere that is both romantic and enchanting.

I see a couple walking by, their arms wrapped around each other, lost in their own world of love and happiness. The sight fills me with a warm sense of contentment, and I can't help but smile at the beauty of it all. I wish that were me and Jack. When I think about Jack, my mind races with questions and doubts. I'm torn between my love for him and my desire for a family. The future feels uncertain and daunting, and I cannot shake off the unease that grips me.

At this moment, I can't help but feel a sense of longing for Jack's presence. The city below me is alive with activity, but I feel like a spectator, disconnected from the world around me. I feel more alone than ever before.

I close the curtain and drop onto the bed.

I can't breathe, so I turn on the ceiling fan. I lie on the bed and watch the fan spin faster. My mind is moving extremely fast too.

Should I tell him?

Will he want to be a part of our child's life?

Or will he walk away from the baby and me?

I decide to call my best friend, Sarah, for advice. As soon as she answers the phone, I blurt out, "Sarah, I'm pregnant. With Jack's baby."

"What? Oh my God. How did you get a relationship with that monster? Are you okay?" Sarah asks, her voice laced with concern.

"I don't know. I don't know if I should tell Jack. He has a no-commitment policy, and I'm afraid he'll walk away," I confess, my voice trembling.

"You should tell him. He deserves to know, and you need his support," Sarah advises.

"But what if he wants nothing to do with us?" I ask, my heart sinking at the thought.

"Then that's his loss. You and your baby deserve better than someone who won't commit," Sarah replies firmly.

I know she's right, but telling Jack still scares me.

I take a deep breath and dial his number.

"Hey there, gorgeous," he says, his tone upbeat and humorous.

I can't help but smile at the sound of it. "Hey, yourself."

The background sounds like Jack's driving, "Where are you heading?" I ask.

"I'm on my way to... a secret place," he says. "Why, what's up?"

"I just wanted to talk to you," I say, feeling a sudden nervousness come over me.

"Is everything okay?" he asks, concern creeping into his voice.

"I don't know," I say, my voice faltering. "The director already told you my performance today wasn't good, right?"

"Yeah," he says, his tone serious. "But you're one of the best actresses I know. You'll get through this."

"I hope so," I say, "But I miss you."

"I miss you too," he says, his voice softening. "Are you feeling sick? Do you need me to bring you anything?"

"No, I'm okay," I say, feeling a sense of warmth spread through me at his concern. "I just wanted to talk to you."

"Well, Olivia, I have a poor connection here. I'll call you back."

"Okay," I say, then I hang up the phone.

Soon, I hear a knock at the door. "Who is this?" I ask.

"Room service." It is an old man's voice.

I open the door and surprisingly find Jack standing there, a massive grin on his face.

How wonderful it is!

"Hey, there, gorgeous," he says, embracing me tightly.

"Hey, you!" I say, feeling a sense of warmth and love spread through me at his touch.

We sit on the sofa together. I lean on Jack's shoulder. "What brought you here?"

"You." Jack pulls me away from his shoulder and scans me carefully. His eyes are full of concern, and I have never heard him talk like this. "James told me you're ill. So, I put off my daily work schedule. Are you sick?"

"Jack, so many questions. You sound like my grandma now." I smile. "But thank you," I say quietly.

"What's up?" Jack stares at me. "Is the shooting too hard? Anything I can do for you?"

I see hope. "Yes, Jack, you can help me. Can you modify the script?"

"Which scene do you want to modify?" Jack grabs his cell phone and is ready to take notes.

"Remove the remaining two fighting scenes. I don't want to run or kick anymore."

"Why?" Jack drops his cell phone on the sofa and stretches his arms out along the back.

"Too hard for me," I reply quietly.

"Olivia, it's the first time you've played a lead role in a feature film. It's hard, but it's the landmark to your success. Show your respect for it and give your best."

"Jack, I'm so tired. I hope to have a little break, a week."

"No, Olivia, everything must be on schedule once we start," he replies decisively.

"I just need to slow down a bit." I see the director's disappointed face again. I do not want to face that embarrassing moment again.

"You're competing with the best. You don't get to stop. You must go full on else you'll be left behind." His voice is firm.

"Jack, I..." I want to tell him I'm carrying his baby, but Jack interrupts me before I finish my words.

"Olivia, you have enormous potential. I will do whatever I can to help you become a superstar, but you need to try independently."

Jack stands up, pulls me up from the sofa, and leads me to the bed.

He hugs me tightly. I know that next, his hand will be inside my pajamas, and his body will be on top of mine. My body is ready for his touch... but I know he can be very rough, and I start worrying about the secret baby... *Jack, whatever you do, please do not hurt our baby.*

Unexpectedly, he just says calmly, "Rest, my poor girl. You must be tired. Tomorrow will be another long day. Get some sleep." Then he picks me up and drops me on my bed.

"Good night." He turns off the lights and leaves.

Looking at the closed door, I suddenly feel so stupid.

I haven't told Jack I'm pregnant. Why do I suddenly have so many useless complaints? Am I missing the best opportunity?

Chapter 10. Jack

The moment I close Olivia's door, I force myself to leave.

When I stood by her bed, I wanted to slip my hands inside her loose pajamas and hold her tiny nipples between my fingers again. I wanted to penetrate her body deeply, over, and over. I would enjoy hearing her pants and moans under me; it turns me on. I could spend my entire night with her like this.

Whenever I put my hands on her warm body and glide along her soft curves, all my troubles and stress disappear. I will never forget how perfect and alluring her firm breasts are in the moonlight.

But I didn't.

Now I'm lying in my own bed, and all I'm thinking about is Olivia. I had a chance to share another steamy night with her—which I have been wanting for a week. Olivia loves me. She will allow me to do anything I want, but I can't. As I looked into her tired eyes, I knew that I couldn't continue down this path.

The curtains are drawn. The room is dark and quiet. The red, green, and yellow flashes of electrical appliances are scattered throughout the room, like thoughts that pop into my mind occasionally.

I notice the changes inside me. I've realized that my attitude towards Olivia had changed substantially. I paid attention to her beautiful body in the past, but now, I care more about her feelings, and I know I needed to put her needs before my own desires. As much as I wanted to continue the passion we shared, I couldn't bear the thought of causing her any more pain or exhaustion.

The physical attraction that had drawn me to her was still present, but now tempered with a deep and heartfelt love that I couldn't deny. How long can I hold out without touching her? I don't know, but I'll find out.

Someday, when Olivia recovers, I'll keep her busy for the entire night. No, one night is not enough, I need a to make love with her a week in a row, until she begs for mercy. With this last thought, I fall asleep. I will let this little beauty pay me back.

Next morning, I wake up by the alarm. It's seven o'clock, and in thirty minutes, I need to join the crew downstairs for breakfast.

I can already smell the food before I walk into the restaurant.

The restaurant is beautifully decorated, with warm lighting and sleek furnishings. As I take a seat at the table, actors greet me, all of them eager for the day ahead.

"So, what's on the schedule for today?" one of the actors asks James eagerly.

"We'll be shooting the final scene in the theater," the director replies, smiling at their enthusiasm.

"The final scene? That's a big one," another actor chimes in.

I nod. "Yes, and we need to make sure it's perfect. The success of the entire project depends on it."

James moves closer to me, and we begin to discuss the details of the upcoming shoot. The conversation is lively and full of energy as we bounce ideas off each other.

"We need to make sure the lighting is just right," James says, his voice confident. "And the camera angles need to be perfect to capture the emotion of the scene."

"Absolutely," I chime in. "And the actors need to be at the top of their game. This is the moment that everything leads up to."

The actors nod in agreement, excitement building within them. The food is delicious.

Everyone is in good spirits.

I glance over at Olivia; I notice that she looks nervous and tense. She is struggling to keep her breakfast down and is visibly nauseous. The director also sees the discomfort on Olivia's face. He clears his throat, but before he can open his mouth, Olivia looks panicked and suddenly jumps up from the table, hurrying towards the restroom. The two actresses sitting closest follow her, clearly concerned.

As they leave the room, I can feel the tension in the air. Something is clearly wrong, and I know that we need to make sure that Olivia is okay.

Then I hear the conversation around the table.

"Morning sickness, huh?" one of the actors chuckles, trying to lighten the mood.

"Yeah, it looks like we have another baby on board," another actress jokes, eliciting laughter from the group.

James looks at me. "Jack, you see, this is what I worry about."

I nod. I have concerns, but I can't say them out loud.

"How long has she been this way?" I ask.

"About a week, since you left," the director shakes his head. "I hope she's just temporarily sick, not—" He stops.

Not pregnant. I know what the rest of the words are.

I hope the same.

Olivia returns to her seat, the two actresses walking beside her. Her face looks very shy and embarrassed.

"I'll go check on her," I say, standing up from the table and heading to Olivia. "Are you okay?" I ask, my voice filled with concern.

There is a long pause before Olivia responds, her voice shaky and weak. "No, I don't think so."

"Okay, we're going to help you get back to your room," I say, trying to sound as reassuring as possible.

"No, I need to finish the shoot," Olivia replies, looking at me.

"You can stay if you need rest." I hope she can stay in the hotel to rest.

"No, I can't cause a delay. I've given James enough problems," Olivia insists.

"Okay, let's move." I turn to the director.

Two hours later, we start shooting on the stage. As the cameras start rolling, the theater transforms into a dazzling display of lights and sound. The stage is set with a backdrop of the Eiffel Tower, beautifully painted in shades of blue and gold. Extras are seated in period clothing adding to the authenticity of the scene.

Olivia takes her place onstage, dressed in a stunning black dress with her hair elegantly styled. As she starts to sing, her voice fills the theater, rich and full of emotion. The stage lights create a beautiful halo around her, highlighting her beauty and talent.

Talented musicians make up the band, each playing their instruments with passion and precision. The sound they create is a beautiful blend of jazz and French chanson, transporting the audience back in time to the streets of 1940s Paris.

As Olivia sings, the camera moves around the theater, capturing the reactions of the audience. The faces of the extras mirror the awe that is within them. Olivia's performance is breathtaking.

The lighting design is exquisite, creating a sense of depth and movement on stage. The shadows and highlights play off each other, adding to the drama and emotion of the scene. Every detail has been carefully considered, from the costumes to the set design, to create a truly immersive and authentic experience.

As the scene ends, the audience erupts in applause, their appreciation for Olivia's performance clear. It is a moment of magic, a moment that captures the essence of the story and the spirit of the time. And as we wrap up filming for the day, I'm filled with pride. We have created something exceptional.

It is so real, so affecting. When I watch Olivia play her role on stage, I feel enormously proud of her.

Then the director comes over to me with an apologetic expression on his face.

"Sorry, Jack—"

"Do not tell me you need to redo it," I interrupt.

"Sorry, we have to redo the scene," he says, his tone urgent.

"What happened?" I ask, concerned.

"One of the camera guys forgot to change the lens for the stage shoot," the director explains, frustration clear in his voice. "We need to get it right if we're going to make this scene work."

"Can Olivia manage it?" I ask, my voice filled with concern. I'm worried about her.

The director considers for a moment before responding. "We'll need to take a break and make sure she's okay," he says, his tone reassuring. "But we must get this shot. It's too important to the film."

I turn to Olivia, who looks tired but determined.

"Are you up for it?" I ask, my voice gentle.

She takes a deep breath before responding. "I can do it," she says, her voice filled with resolve. "Let's get it done."

With Olivia's agreement, we take a break to regroup and prepare for the reshoot. The crew rushes to reset the stage and make the necessary changes to the camera equipment. The tension in the air is palpable, as everyone knows that this reshoot could make or break the success of the entire film.

As we prepare for the reshoot, I try to keep Olivia's spirits up, offering her words of encouragement and support. "You've got this," I say confidently. "You're a pro, and you can handle anything that comes your way."

With renewed determination, Olivia takes her place on stage once again, ready to give it her all. The camera rolls, and she begins to sing, her voice soaring with emotion and passion. The crew moves around the stage with precision, capturing every moment of the scene.

I see the director nod in satisfaction. "That's the one," he says, a smile of relief spreading across his face.

I turn to Olivia, who is looking exhausted but proud. "You did it," I say, my voice filled with admiration. "You gave it your all, and it shows."

We gather around the monitors to review the footage. However, before we can even begin, Olivia falls to the ground, her body shaking uncontrollably. I rush to her side as the producer manager calls for emergency help.

The next few minutes are a blur of activity as we wait for the ambulance to arrive. I can feel panic rising within me as I watch Olivia struggle to breathe. The director and crew work quickly to make sure that she is safe and comfortable, doing everything they can to help.

Finally, the ambulance arrives. I ride with her in the ambulance, and tell the others stay where they are to finish shooting.

On the way to hospital my heart pounds with fear and anxiety. I can feel the weight of the situation bearing down on me. This is not how I imagined the day would go.

When we arrive at the hospital the doctors rush to Olivia's side, performing a battery of tests and exams. I wait outside the door anxiously as they work, my mind racing with worry. I can't bear the thought of anything happening to her.

Hours pass before I finally receive news from the doctors. "Olivia is stable," the doctor says, her tone reassuring. "She is pregnant, but she and her baby will be okay."

Relief floods through me. I'm so grateful that Olivia is safe and, on the mend, but I only want to hear the first half of the sentence.

As I walk into the patient's temporary room, the first thing I notice is Olivia's nervous face.

Nurses are passing by in the hall. I pull the blue curtain around and close us inside, so she can have more peace.

Olivia looks at me and smiles softly. "Now, you know my secret, I don't have to worry about how to tell you anymore."

I sit next to her bed and hold her hands.

"Olivia, I love you," I say, my voice soft. "And I'll support you through this. But I must be honest about my rules."

Olivia looks up at me, sadness filling her face.

"You knew clearly in the beginning, I have rules," I say, my voice firm but gentle. "No commitment, no family, no children. I need to focus on my creation, to produce the best movies in the world."

Olivia nods. "I see," she says, her voice filled with a mix of disappointment and acceptance.

"I hope you can understand," I say, my voice full of emotion. "I want to be with you, but I also have to be true to myself."

Olivia takes my hand in hers, offering me a small smile of support. "I understand," she says, her voice filled with love and support.

"I also want you understand, I don't want anyone to know about our relationship. I don't want to mix my personal life with business."

"Sure," Olivia agrees.

"I can't allow anything to block me from success," I say, my voice unwavering. "I know it's not fair to you, but I have to be true to my goals." My voice is cold and firm, reflecting the importance of my career.

Olivia nods. "I understand," she says again, her voice filled with sadness.

"Good. I hope you can forgive me," I say, my voice softening slightly. "I don't want to lose you."

Olivia takes a deep breath before responding. "I forgive you," she says, her voice filled with emotion. "But you're selfish, and I can't make any promises about our future." She pulls her hands away from mine.

I nod, a sense of grief filling me. "I understand," I say, my voice barely above a whisper.

I stand up and walk to the window. As I look out, watching the cars and passengers going about their day, I'm reminded of the importance of time. Each person has the same twenty-four hours in a day, but how we use that time can make all the difference.

I turn and face Olivia.

"God is fair," I say, my voice thoughtful. "But what we spend our time on can make a huge difference, not only in our personal lives, but also in the contributions we can make to the world."

Olivia nods, a small smile crossing her face. "You're right." Her voice is full of gratitude. "We all have to make choices about how we use our time," she says.

"We get to make difficult choices in life." My voice is firm.

My cell phone rings again. It's an important call, and I know I must answer.

I look at Olivia, she forces a smile at me. "Jack, you should go. I'll be fine."

I answer the call as I open the blue curtain and head to the hallway.

I'm glad I made the right decision. *I must keep my rules.*

Chapter 11. Olivia

Later in the evening Nancy, the production manager, picks me up from the hospital.

On the way to my apartment, Nancy tells me I can take a day off tomorrow. James hopes I get well soon.

It gets dark, and I am amazed by the beautiful street view under the streetlights. I see lovers holding hands, walking along the street; outside Starbucks, the tables are packed, and I can hear a group of young people's laughter...

Why do these happy scenes only bring me sadness?

When we stop at a red traffic light, Nancy asks, "Are you okay?" She is about fifty years old, has been divorced three times, and is now single. She must have exceptional sensitivity to my hidden feelings.

"I'm okay." I remember what Jake told me; he doesn't want anyone to discover our relationship.

I open my apartment door and turn on the light.

"Wow, your place is so nice." Nancy sighs. "It's good to be young. My little nest is full of antiques, all grandma stuff."

"I like simple," I reply shortly. I'm in no mood to talk.

Everything is familiar—the desk and bookshelves, the couch and coffee table are all modern style. I love their simple cut and sharp look, but now my feelings are strange, as if my life has changed forever.

I'm no longer the girl with a warm heart full of desire. I'm a future single mom.

After the production manager leaves, I go to the balcony, letting the light breeze blow through my hair. I'm lost in thought, wondering what the future holds for me now that my life has taken such a drastic turn. I sit there for what feels like hours, watching the city come alive under the glow of the streetlights. The sounds of cars and people fill the air, reminding me of the world outside my little balcony.

The busier they are, the lonelier I am.

I remember one joke my brother Paul made. "Jack is extraordinary. He is a rock. It can be scalding hot in the sun or as cold as ice in the moonlight. However, at any time, he can smash the head of anyone who stands in his way. "

I miss Paul. It's been a long time since I've seen him. I grab my phone and dial his number, hoping to catch him at a suitable time.

"Hey, Sis!" Paul answers, his voice full of energy. "What's up?"

"I miss you," I say, my voice filled with longing. "Can we talk for a bit?"

"Sure thing!" Paul says, his tone cheerful. "But I have some good news to share first!"

"What is it?" I ask, my curiosity piqued.

"Jane's pregnant!" Paul exclaims, his voice full of excitement. "We just found out today. She's been pregnant for about two months now!"

I can hear the joy in his voice, and my heart fills with happiness for my brother and his wife. "Congratulations!" I say, my voice filled with joy.

"Yeah, we're pretty excited," Paul says. "I'm busy cooking dinner right now. Jane can eat a whole cow, you know."

I laugh at his joke, picturing my brother trying to keep up with his pregnant wife's appetite. "How's Jane doing?" I ask, wanting to know more.

"She's doing great!" Paul says, his tone proud. "She's a bit picky about her food, but I'm learning to make all her favorites."

Just then, Jane joins the call, her voice filled with laughter and excitement. "Hey!" she exclaims. "I'm so happy to talk to you!"

"Congratulations! I can't wait to meet the little one!"

"Thanks!" Jane replies, her tone full of gratitude. "We're already designing the baby's room. But we do not know if this is a boy or a girl, so we can't decide on the room color. It's going to be amazing!"

As I listen to Paul and Jane talk about their plans, my heart fills with happiness for them. But I can't help feeling a tinge of sadness too. I am living in a different world, with a secret baby and a feeling of loneliness that I can't seem to shake. I hug my shoulders and curl up in a ball on the chair.

I can't tell Paul my secret. Not yet at least. Also, I must keep my promise to Jack. I can't tell my brother about my relationship with his best friend. I don't want to spoil Paul and Jane's happiness or take away from the joy of their news.

"Sis, food's on the table. Got to go."

"Enjoy your meal."

I go to shower. When I'm finished, I hear my phone buzzing with a message from Paul and Jane. They want to share lunch with me tomorrow, and I can hear the excitement in their voices even through text.

I hesitate at first. I'm still grappling with my own struggles and secrets, and I don't want to bring them into their joy and excitement.

I don't know, I type back, my fingers hesitating over the keys.

Then, Jane calls. "Olivia, come over, please."

"I'm not really feeling up to it. I'm tired from the filming."

But Paul and Jane are persistent. They want to see me, to share in their big news. And as I listen to their happy voices, I can't help but feel a sense of longing and hope.

"Come on," Jane urges, her tone cheerful. "It'll be fun. We'll make your favorite food!"

Slowly, I feel myself relenting. It would be good to spend time with Paul and Jane and share their happiness and love.

"Okay," I say, my fingers trembling with excitement. "I'll come over."

The following day, I arrive at my brother's home just before noon. Before I even walk in, I notice the change. The flower bed has new landscaping, with colorful blooms in the sunshine. I cannot help but smile at the sight of it.

As I walk in, Jane greets me at the entry, her arms open wide in welcome. "Welcome, Sis!" she exclaims, delighted. "Come on in!"

I step inside, and I'm struck by the change of the interior decoration. Elegant creamy curtains have replaced the busy floral curtains of before, and the space feels brighter and more open. It's all Jane's doing, I can tell.

"How do you feel?" Jane asks, a twinkle in her eye. "Do you like my redecorating?"

I can't help but laugh. "It's beautiful," I say, my voice full of sincerity. "You have a real talent for design."

Paul chimes in, his tone light and teasing. "Yeah, she's been driving me crazy with all her home improvement projects. I'm only glad she's finally done."

We all laugh at his joke, and I feel warmth and happiness. Moments like these remind me of the joy and love of the simple things in life. As we sit down to lunch, the cheerful atmosphere continues. Paul and Jane are in high spirits, and the conversation flows quickly and effortlessly. As we eat, we discuss all sorts of things, from our favorite foods to plans. And as we talk, I can't help but notice the beautiful decorations inside the dining room. The walls are a warm, inviting color, and elegant art pieces and photographs adorn them.

Suddenly, the conversation turns back to the topic of children. "So," Paul says, his tone playful. "What do you think we're going to have?"

Jane grins. "I want a boy," she says, her voice excitedly. "As handsome as you, Paul."

Paul chuckles. "Nope, I want a girl," he says, teasing. "As beautiful as you, Jane. That way, I'll be surrounded by two attractive females. One brings me food, and one brings me wine."

We all laugh at his joke. It's moments like these that remind me of the power of love and family, and this is the life I want to have. As we continue chatting over lunch, Paul starts questioning me about my latest project.

"How goes the filming?" he asks.

"Good," I reply shortly. This is what I was trying to avoid. I don't want to go down this road. I need a little break from work.

Unfortunately, Jane joins the conversation. She turns to me with a curious expression. "What's it like making a movie?" she asks, her tone full of interest. "What's the process like?"

I take a deep breath, feeling a sense of excitement and passion welling up inside of me. "It's amazing," I say. "There's so much that goes into it, from the scriptwriting to the casting to the actual filming. It's a true collaboration, and it takes hard work and dedication to make it happen."

Jane asks, "Olivia, how is Jack doing? Can you get any support from him?"

I glance over at Paul, and I see Paul's expression turns serious.

"Listen," Paul says, his tone cautionary. "Jack's my best friend, but he's also a bit of a wild card. You need to be careful around him, okay?"

I nod, feeling a sense of gratitude for Paul's concern. "I will," I say, "I'll be careful."

Paul then notices that I look a bit down and asks me "Is the job too tough? You look tired."

I shake my head sadly. "It's not that," I say softly. "It's just... something is going on that's been weighing on my mind."

Paul's expression turns sympathetic, and he reaches for my hand. "What is it?" he asks, his tone full of concern.

I take a deep breath, feeling a sense of vulnerability. But I cannot tell Paul my secret.

"It's tough to be a lead actress," I lie.

"Olivia, we're proud of you. Jack is too tough to offer you any favors just because you're my sister. You're an independent girl." Paul smiles at me.

He refills his glass with red wine, then holds it up and says, "Keep collaborating with Jack and you'll have career success and endless challenges. Jack always challenges the boundaries, pushes the limits. That's why we're buddies."

Paul drinks all the wine, and his face turns red. "Sis, keep your distance from Jack. Never get in his car. Jack is a brilliant businessman but a worse playboy."

Jane's face shows surprise. Paul looks at Jane and explains, "He changes girlfriends faster than his underwear. He treats women the same as he treats his car."

"That's horrible," Jane yells. "How can he have no respect for women? How can you have such a crappy friend?"

Paul puts his glass down and spins it. "Jack is not crappy. He's a genius. He can't just belong to any one woman, even if she is a queen."

I pick up a napkin, wipe my lips, and ask, "Paul, you're a genius too. How can you have a happy family?"

Paul laughs. "Sis, I grew up in a loving family and met my sweet Jane, so I want a dozen kids. Jack grew up in a cold, wealthy family. His mother died when he was young, and he does not feel warm about family life."

"What if someday Jack meets his sweet girl? Do you think he may want to have a family too?"

Paul shakes his head. "Olivia, Jack has met a hundred sweet girls who are all beautiful. I cannot picture Jack sitting by the fireplace to read a children's book to his kids."

"What is the longest relationship he has had with a woman?" I ask.

"Olivia, Jack does not need to report his private life to me. I guess it would not be more than a month."

I lower my head. *Paul, you're wrong. I've been with Jack for much longer than a month, and he still does not want to lose me.*

"Why?" Paul looks into my eyes. "Why do you care so much about Jack's personal life?"

I smile at my brother. "He's the producer. I should know him."

As I answer my brother, I look into his bright eyes. Paul is a genius too. Paul and Jack have a lot in common. They understand each other so well. But they have a different opinion about family life.

Paul needs a wife and a dozen kids. Jack only needs freedom.

And as we finish our lunch and say our goodbyes in the hall, Paul puts his hand on my shoulder. "Listen," he says, his tone serious, "I know this business can be tough, but I want you to know we're here for you."

"No matter what happens, we'll always be here to support you," Jane says, hugging me.

I feel a lump forming in my throat as I look at my brother and sister-in-law. Their love and support mean everything to me.

"Thank you," I say, my voice full of emotion. "Thank you for everything."

With my family's love and support, I know that anything is possible. I will always have a home and a place of belonging, no matter what the future holds.

After leaving Paul's home, I drive to the park instead of returning to my apartment.

A canopy of green leaves shades the bench beneath it now.

On that long wooden bench, Jack took off my black evening dress on that full-moon night. I gave myself unreservedly to him again.

As I sit under the tree again, I can feel the warmth of the summer sun on my skin. The grass is a vibrant green, and the trees are full and lush. The sound of children playing in the distance fills the air, and I can see couples walking hand in hand along the lakeshore.

But my thoughts keep returning to Jack. I remember the passion and intensity of our steamy night together, how he made me feel alive and free. But at the same time, I feel guilt and shame. I am carrying his child and must face the consequences of our actions.

That night I was a fanatical girl, eager to unconditionally dedicate the love I had accumulated for many years to my lover; today, I am a mother-to-be, and what I think about most is not my emotional entanglements but how to make the best arrangements for myself and the baby inside me.

I grew up.

Lost in thought, I hear a voice calling out to me as I sit there. It's a little girl, about five years old, and she's holding a pink balloon in her hand, her red curly hair makes her look like a cute doll.

"Hi, there!" she says, her tone full of excitement. "Want to play with me?"

I smile, feeling a sense of warmth and joy in my heart. Amid my confusion and doubt, this little girl has reminded me of the simple pleasures of life and the beauty that surrounds us every day.

"Yes, I would love to play with you," I say, my voice enthusiastic. At that moment, I feel the relief of motherhood, and I can see myself playing in the grass with my own children in the future.

No matter Jack's choice, I will choose to keep my baby.

Chapter 12. Jack

Since I left the hospital, I haven't seen or talked to Olivia in two days. I miss her. I have been crazily working over thirty hours without a break, and it's been extremely tense. Now I drive back home in the dark in a cheerful mood.

I just closed two big deals. I feel good about it. There was a lot of shit to wade through, but I made it. I brought two big investors on board, and the company is better off. That's what matters.

I know Olivia will want to hear all about it. She's always supported me, even when I'm grumpy and irritable. But I'm not in the mood for chitchat right now. I need to decompress after all the stress of these deals. Tomorrow will be another busy day.

When I arrive home, I collapse onto my couch and turn on the TV. It's just background noise really since I'm too tired to pay attention to anything. What's the next thing I need to do? I want to check my schedule on my cell phone, but my eyes feel heavy and dry. So, I close my eyes to take a break. The last thing I remember is the music on the TV.

While the music plays, Olivia stands on the stage of the grand theater. The theater is alive with energy and anticipation in the 1940s. She wears a stunning silver gown that sparkles under the dimmed lights around the stage. I need to tell James about this. Why is it a silver gown? The black will better contrast her white skin. I look around. The theater's decoration is lavish, with intricate gold detailing adorning the walls and chandeliers hanging from the ceiling, casting a warm glow across the audience. The air is thick with the smell of fresh flowers and polished wood, adding to the magic of the night.

I turn back to the stage and focus on Olivia's performance. I need to make sure everything runs smoothly. The lights around the stage dim. A single spotlight shines down on Olivia, illuminating her as she begins to sing. The lights are perfect. I feel satisfied. Olivia's voice fills the theater, rich and full, echoing off the walls and reaching the hearts of everyone in attendance. She is even better as a singer than an actress. At least *I* think so.

As she sings, the backdrops behind her change, transporting the audience to various places and times. They take a journey to a grand ballroom with walls adorned with gold and silver and a floor that shines like a mirror. Then, to a dark forest with towering trees that cast shadows.

I come backstage, behind the backdrops, and wait for Olivia. There are layers of backdrops, and I pick the one in the middle. No one will need to pass through here.

As Olivia's song ends, the lights around the stage grow brighter, illuminating the entire theater. The audience erupts into thunderous applause, their cheers filling the air. Olivia bows, then walks to the side of the stage.

"Olivia," I call, my voice low and deep.

Olivia runs to me; her face is still extremely excited.

"Jack, I can sing," she whispers into my ear.

Her breasts are lifted and pushed together; the top half exposed by the plunging neckline of the costume. It's so tempting.

I pull the back zipper of her dress down to her waist at once, and her entire upper body is completely exposed. Next, I deftly undo her bra, throwing it far backstage. In the dim light, I see her pink nipples again hardening before I can pinch them. They are ready for me to bite.

"No, Jack, it's too dangerous. So many people around here." Olivia's voice is incredibly soft. When she says no, her arms circle my neck to pull my head down to her breast.

I carry her to the corner, entirely covered by layers of the dusty backdrop. Along the way, I suck harder and harder on her tits. Then I put her on the dark red floor. The golden floor-to-ceiling backdrops separate us from the outside world. The orchestra in the pit is playing fierce music, and I jump on her body suddenly. I can't control myself anymore. My movements go with the strong rhythm of the instruments. I thrust into Olivia's warmth over and over.

"Need more?" I ask when I enter her.

"Yes."

"Want it harder?" My hands grab her breasts, and my fingers pinch her delicate nipples simultaneously.

"Yes."

Her body keeps moving under me.

"Do you want to try a different way?"

"Sure." As she says so, I've already flipped her and attack her from the side.

Olivia moans louder beneath me, but it's completely drowned out by the deafening music. I watch her tits turn pink in my palms. What a wonderful feeling!

"If this is the end of the world, it is the only thing I want to do," I joke to Olivia as I flip her body to face me.

Suddenly, I see a particularly terrifying expression on Olivia's face.

"Jack!" she cries out in horror. Her finger points to the roof.

I look up and see a man on the stage's roof, standing on a beam and taking pictures of us with a camera. The beam is cracking, and about to break and hit us. I pick up Olivia and escape to a safe place. On the side of the stage, we bump into the director, James.

"Jack, Olivia, what happened?" James asks, his face changing from surprised to anger.

Before I can reply I hear a loud bang, the beam snaps and hits the ground hard, and the man falls in front of us with his camera. Olivia starts screaming. The audience can hear her voice, and more noise comes from the front of the theater.

I suddenly wake up.

The TV is playing a war movie, and a woman is screaming. It's just a dream. A good and evil dream. I turn off the TV, head to my bedroom, and throw myself in bed. Before I fall asleep, I still feel shocked. The dream was so absolute. It made me feel ashamed. I was as rough as a beast when I made love to Olivia, and I never really respected her feelings. I'm trampling on her love for me. It should never happen again. Absolutely not.

The next day, I wake up feeling refreshed. This should be a better day. On my way to work, I see the flashing yellow light; a school zone is ahead. There's a lengthy line of cars ahead. I hit the brakes hard and reduce my speed to twenty miles per hour. It's an excellent time to chat with Olivia via speakerphone. I need to know what's going on with the "secret baby" situation.

"Hey there, Olivia. Just wanted to say hi and see how you're doing." I sound casual.

Olivia's voice is soft on the other end of the line. "I'm fine. I visited Paul over the weekend."

I smile. Paul is my best friend, and I know how close he is to Olivia. "That's great. How's he doing?" I ask.

Olivia's voice brightens. "He's doing well. And guess what? His wife is two months pregnant."

"Wow." I feel a surge of happiness for Paul. Paul's always been a family man; I know he'll make a great dad. But then I remember Olivia's own pregnancy, and my mood changes rapidly.

From a distance, I look at the long motorcade on the road in front of the elementary school's gate. The parents sitting in their cars are dropping off their children at school. They wait in this line every day for years and years.

What a horrible existence. I can't let this be my life. Absolutely not.

"That's great news. I'm happy for Paul and Jane," I say, sounding sincere. But inside, I'm panicking. I'm a free man. I can never turn myself into a family man. I pause.

Olivia senses my hesitation. "Are you okay?" she asks, her voice soft.

I take a deep breath, trying to compose myself. "Yeah, I'm fine. Just busy with work, you know."

No reply from Olivia. It's obvious she isn't convinced. I feel a pang of guilt. I know I'm not doing enough to help Olivia through this.

"One thing I can promise you: you will not be alone," I say, my voice strained.

Olivia just sighs. "I understand all your rules. But I feel like you're shutting me out."

"I'm not shutting you out. I love you, and I need you." When I say so, the dream returns to me again.

Olivia just sighs. "Okay. Just promise me you'll talk to me soon."

I finish the conversation before entering the school zone, feeling a mix of emotions. I must find a solution before Olivia's figure turns into that of a pregnant woman.

I go into the office building, feeling good about yesterday's success. I'm even in a good mood when I see Emily in the break room. She is adding sugar to her coffee.

"Hey, how are you feeling? You look happy today," Emily says, smiling brightly, but all her beauty is gone now that I know her personality.

"I'm fine," I mutter, grabbing coffee and leaving. My instinct tells me to keep my distance from this sneaky woman.

I take my coffee and walk to my office. The entire morning I'm busy. At noon, when I head to the studio dining hall, my hunger reminds me I have yet to have breakfast. I enter the dining hall, scowling as I grab a tray and head for the buffet line. I'm not in the mood for small talk, but I know I won't find peace here. Many will take that opportunity to approach me, pitch a script, or recommend an actor, the only difference being what they want from me.

Sure enough, Sarah, Olivia's best friend, spots me and makes a beeline for my table.

"Hey, Jack. How's your day going?" she asks, a smirk on her face.

I grunt in response, taking a bite of my sandwich. "Fine." I don't like the way she smiles. She is, at most, a third-rate actress, and she can't even pretend to smile in front of her boss.

Sarah rolls her eyes. "Come on, don't be like that. You know I'm Olivia's best friend."

I just stare at her, unamused. No one here would dare to talk to me like this.

"So, what's the deal with the secret baby?" she asks, her voice low.

I feel my cheeks flush with embarrassment. I don't want anyone else to hear about this.

"Stay away from me." I stare at her; my voice is low but firm.

Sarah shakes her head. "Olivia is afraid to talk to you. I'm not. Do you want to take responsibility for the baby?"

I can feel the eyes of other diners on us. I must shut this conversation down. I stand up to leave. But Sarah needs to finish. "Well, you can't just ignore it."

That's when I notice Emily sitting at a nearby table, listening to our conversation.

But it's too late. Emily has heard everything, a sly smile on her face.

I leave the dining hall and head to my office. I slam my office door, feeling furious. I can't believe Olivia broke her promise about keeping the baby a secret.

I dial her number, my hands shaking with anger. "Olivia, what the hell? You promised to keep this between us. Why did you tell Sarah?"

There's a pause at the other end of the line before Olivia speaks. "I'm sorry. It was on the day I found out I was pregnant. I was scared and didn't know what to do, so I called Sarah for advice."

I feel a twinge of guilt. I know how important Sarah is to Olivia. But that doesn't excuse her from causing this problem.

"You should have talked to me first," I say, my voice low but still angry.

"I know, and I'm sorry. But you must understand, I was terrified," Olivia says, her voice shaky.

I take a deep breath, trying to calm myself down. "I understand. But you must promise me that you won't tell anyone else. This could damage my reputation."

"I promise," Olivia says, her voice firm.

"Where are you? Can we meet?" I need to make arrangements to support her.

"No, I'm on set. I still have five scenes to shoot, then I'll return to the studio."

I hang up the phone, feeling a little better.

In the afternoon, I join the celebration party for Alex's crew. They've just completed the war movie, and everyone is extremely excited.

As I drink wine with Alex and watch people sing and dance, I feel uneasy. I should be working, not partying. I have urgent emails that need reply. One's from the bank.

I look at my watch and turn to Alex. "It's 4:45. The bank will close in fifteen minutes. I've got to reach the manager today."

"I understand," Alex says. "Come back when you finish. I have something I need to discuss with you."

"Deal," I say.

I slip away from the crowd, finding a quiet spot in an office nearby. I pull out my phone and start responding to those urgent messages. When I work, the music and the noise all fade around me. I make a very quick phone call with the bank manager first, then send text messages and respond to emails.

That's when Emily walks in, a wicked smile on her face. "Hey there, Boss. What are you doing hiding out here?"

I keep typing. "Working."

Emily just laughs. "Oh, come on. Don't be like that. I have something to show you. I know you must like it." Before I can say anything, she starts undressing, revealing her body. "If Olivia can get the lead role by having sex with you, why can't I do the same?" she asks, a sly look in her eyes.

I feel sick to my stomach. "Stop it. Get out." But Emily just keeps going, getting louder and more insistent. "Sneaky." I leave.

Suddenly, I hear Emily screaming behind the closed door. "Help! Help me, please!"

A group of people rush out of the party and meet me in the hall. Some run into the office and see Emily crying without clothes on.

They're shocked and angry.

I know I've fallen into the trap set by Emily.

Daniel, the director, is there, his face red with anger. "What the hell is going on here?" he shouts.

I've never seen Daniel angry. He never made a sound when he was in front of me. From his attitude, he and Emily must have an unusual relationship.

The hallway becomes crowded. The party room is empty now. Emily appears from the office with disheveled hair and clothes, looking like a victim. Many sympathetic eyes are on her. An actress nearby lends Emily support as if she's too weak to stand.

Should I explain?

No. It would only cause me more trouble.

It would be hard for any decent person to imagine what Emily could be capable of. She would do anything to the point of trading herself and framing others to reach her purpose.

So, I ask, "What time is it?" A few people start looking at their cell phones.

"Alex," I call to the director, "what's the time now?"

"Four fifty-five, Jack," Alex replies. His voice is as calm as usual. He may be the one that knows Emily more than anyone else here.

I look at Daniel. "Call the police, will you?"

My request must be unexpected to Daniel. He looks at me, "Sure, Boss, if you request, you will take the consequences."

I see Alex nod at me. He must understand what's happening.

Daniel gives me a hostile look and starts calling the police.

"Daniel, please, don't call the police. Let Jack go," Emily cries out to stop Daniel from calling the police.

Daniel does not want to let me go. He finishes calling the police in full view of everyone.

Soon, two police cars roar up, and when four police officers appear in front of the crowd with serious expressions, I say, "Officer, thank you for coming in time. I demand immediate forensics. This Emily falsely accused me of sexually assaulting her."

Then, I tell the police officer: "Alex can be my witness. I left the party venue and went to the office next door to work at 4:45; I appeared in this corridor ten minutes later, and all these onlookers saw me. As for what I did in those ten minutes in between, phone calls, emails, and texts can tell you. I was working."

Alex steps forward and says firmly, "I can testify."

"Officer, I request a sexual assault evidence kit from Emily. My lawyer will ask for a written report."

When Emily leaves in despair under the escort of the police officer, I tell Daniel, "Emily will not have any more job opportunities here. As for you, if Emily misled you, you're welcome to stay. If you want to leave, I will send you off."

Alex steps forward. "Let's move back to the party."

Soon, the music starts again.

Sarah comes up to me. When we dance together, she says, "Now I understand why Olivia is so crazy about you."

Sarah is quiet the rest of the time as we dance, but we're both thinking about the same thing: Olivia and her secret baby.

Chapter 13. Olivia

It's the beginning of August, and I'm so glad to return to the studio. Now I can see Jack more often. Hollywood is buzzing with activity. Walking down the streets, I'm surrounded by glitz and glamour. Billboards for upcoming movies and TV shows tower over me, each more impressive than the last. The air is warm and balmy, with a slight breeze that carries the scent of blooming flowers.

Palm trees and expensive cars line the streets, all shining in the bright California sun. People crowd the sidewalks, eager to make their mark on the entertainment industry.

Everything is so familiar, but I am excited because Jack is here.

I pass by studios and production houses, each one bustling with activity. I can hear cameras whirring and actors rehearsing their lines. It's a constant reminder of the frenetic pace of Hollywood, where every day is a new opportunity to create something magical.

When I return to the studio with my crew, I feel I'm back home with a group of my friends. We became closer when we ran in the woods and chatted near the camping fire. Next, we will complete the rest of the shooting for the movie inside the studio.

I meet James at the studio entry, heading to a meeting.

"Olivia, Jack called a meeting. The assistant director is in charge here. I'm pleased with the shots we've taken so far. Keep up the magnificent work."

"Sure," I reply with confidence.

As I slip into character, freedom and exhilaration are with me. I can let go of myself and become someone else entirely. I'm much better than I was two months ago.

The male lead is holding a massive bottle of water. He looks more like a friendly mailman without the German officer's uniform.

"Hey, Ms. Spy, our hero, has arrived." He is delighted to see me. He was a shy guy when we met, but not anymore.

"Hi, Mr. Officer; I can't save you if it's real life. Instead, I can get you killed a hundred times." I laugh. "I've never kicked anyone, not even a dog."

The male lead drops the water bottle and walks over. He is charming and talented, and we have great chemistry on camera. We work seamlessly together, each one feeding off the other's energy. We need to practice a little before shooting.

Later in the evening, when I pack up my things and say goodbye to the crew, my phone rings, and I see that it's Sarah calling.

"Hey there, Sarah. How's it going?" I ask as I pick up my script.

Sarah's voice is warm and inviting. "Hi, Olivia. It's been a while. I'm wondering if you're free for dinner tonight. I'd love to catch up."

I feel a surge of excitement. It's been too long since I've seen Sarah, and I'm eager to hear about what's been happening in her life.

"Absolutely. That sounds great. Where should we meet?" I ask.

Sarah suggests an Italian restaurant in town, and I agree. We plan to meet at 7:00 p.m., and I hang up the phone feeling a sense of anticipation.

As I walk out of the studio, I look around, hoping I can see Jack somewhere, but he's not there. I walk to the parking lot. On my way, I can't help but think about Jack. He's been the highlight of my time here at the studio, even though we must keep our relationship secret. I wish I could be open about my relationship with Jack to share our happiness with the world. But just the thought of seeing him again fills me with excitement and anticipation. I can't help but feel a sense of longing to date openly.

But I know that's not possible, not in this industry, not with all the scrutiny and judgment that comes with being in the public eye. So, I'll have to keep our relationship a secret, sneaking glances at him whenever we're in the same room. And even though it's not ideal, just seeing his face in the dining hall makes everything worth it.

I arrive at the restaurant at 7:00 p.m., feeling a sense of anticipation. Sarah is already there, waiting for me at a cozy table near the window.

Sarah gives me a warm hug.

"Hey, Sarah, you look great," I say. I like her new skirt. "You should save this nice skirt for dating."

"No luck. I just broke with the latest one last week." Sarah makes a sad face at me. I know she's joking.

As I sit down, I can't help but admire the decor. Exposed brick and old-world paintings line the walls giving the space a rustic yet elegant feel. White linens drape the tables set with delicate glassware and silverware.

"Wow, nice place, good pick." I smile at my friend.

The scent of garlic and tomato fills the air, making my mouth water. I glance at the menu and see a variety of classic Italian dishes, from homemade pasta to fresh seafood.

"Will you be okay with this type of food?" Sarah asks.

"The vomiting period is over. Now I can eat everything on the menu." I call the waiter and start making my order. "I think I'm going to go for the lasagna," I say, my mouth already watering.

"That sounds delicious. I think I'll go for the seafood linguine." Sarah nods in agreement.

As we wait for our food to arrive, we catch up.

Sarah sips her coffee, then looks at me, saying, "You must know Emily's story, right?"

"What do you mean?" I feel confused.

"Emily set a trap for Jack."

"Is it an awful story?" I ask. "Tell me. What happened?" I suddenly feel tension. I know how bad Emily can be.

"So, I guess Jack hasn't told you, right?" Sarah shakes her head. "Jack is not an ordinary man."

"Tell me, please." I can't wait anymore.

"Emily is a sneaky woman. She thought she was beautiful, and Jack would be interested in her body, so she snuck into an office where Jack was working," Sarah says, shaking her head. Water splashes out of my glass. How dare Emily try to manipulate Jack like that?

"And what did Jack do?" I ask, my voice tense.

Sarah's expression turns serious. "Emily undressed herself and showed her body to Jack, but Jack turned her down, of course." Sarah laughs.

"Don't stop. Go on," I urge.

"But Emily didn't take no for an answer. She screamed like someone was killing her, and we all heard it from the party room. We rushed out to save her, but it was too late."

My heart sinks. I can't believe Emily would stoop so low as to accuse Jack of rape.

"And then what happened?" I ask, my voice barely above a whisper.

Sarah takes a deep breath. "Jack is a super smart and tough guy. He knew what Emily was up to, so he turned her over to the police."

I look at Sarah, waiting.

Sarah continues, "He didn't argue or waste a minute. He fixed the bitch and kicked her out of the studio."

"Thank you, Sarah. I'm relieved to hear that Jack's fine. It's really thrilling."

Sarah nods in agreement. "I know. But he's a survivor. He's not going to let anyone bring him down."

"No, Jack's not a survivor. Jack is the one who's unbreakable." I smile proudly.

Our food arrives, and we fall silent, lost in the flavors and textures of the cuisine. The lasagna is rich and flavorful, and the seafood linguine is fresh and tender.

Sarah lays her forks into the plate and asks, "Will Jack want to be your baby's father?" I smile, but don't answer her question. "Your body will start to show in less than a month. How will you face people?"

"Sarah, I don't want to talk about this." I feel pain inside, but I must keep the promise to Jack.

"Olivia, wake up. You're making a huge mistake. Do you have any plans for your life? Your career, your family?"

"Sarah, I know what I need to do. Please don't worry about me."

Sarah leans over the table, gets closer to me, and looks into my eyes.

"Olivia, I can feel your pain. I've been there before. There are so many things you'll deal with, but you have no clue at this point."

I shake my head. I tell myself: I am a grown woman. I am brave. I dare to face future challenges.

Sarah senses my thoughts. Sometimes she knows me better than I know myself.

"Olivia, you can sacrifice yourself. But you shouldn't sacrifice your baby's life. As a mother, you should choose wisely for your baby."

I sit there. I can't eat any more. There are so many memories that come to my mind. Some are so sweet, but some so bitter. I can still feel Jack's breath, his touch, and hear his words. Jack can be fire or ice, but he's the man I love.

Suddenly, I notice Sarah is looking at the doorway. She is alert.

I look at the entry and see Daniel, the director and Emily walk in, hand in hand. My heart sinks as I realize the implications of their relationship.

Sarah leans in close to me, her eyes filled with concern. "Emily must be using Daniel to get back at Jack. We need to be careful."

I shoot Emily a disdainful glance. How could Emily be so heartless as to use someone else's feelings to hurt Jack? It's unforgivable.

"How can she hurt Jack?" I ask.

"I don't know. You and I will never imagine how bad Emily can be." Sarah bites her lip.

"And what about me?" I ask, my voice trembling. "Do you think she'll try to hurt me too?"

Sarah nods, her expression serious. "I wouldn't put it past her. We need to be ready for anything."

I take a deep breath, trying to steady my nerves. I know I need to be strong for our baby.

"You'll be okay. You've got me. We'll stick together and make sure that Emily can't hurt you," Sarah says, her voice firm.

"Thank you."

Emily and Daniel are giggling together after seating.

She's hanging on to his every word, nodding and smiling at his jokes, and touching his arm every chance she gets. It's clear that she's trying to please him, to manipulate him into giving her more screen time or a better role. And it's not just me who sees it—Sarah is watching her too, her expression darkening by the second.

I try to ignore Emily and focus on my meal. But every time I glance in her direction, I feel anger and disgust. How could she be so shameless and willing to use others to get ahead?

As Sarah and I go back to eating, we hear footsteps approaching our table. I turn to see Emily, her eyes shining with malice.

"Well, well, well. Look who we have here. The spy and her little friend," Emily says, her voice dripping with sarcasm.

I feel a surge of anger rising in my chest. I don't want to deal with Emily's games, not now, not ever.

"What do you want, Emily?" I ask, my voice cold.

Emily smiles, her eyes darting between Sarah and me. "Oh, nothing much. I just wanted to come over and say hi to my two favorite people in the studio."

I roll my eyes, feeling a sense of disgust. Emily's words are ugly and full of hidden meanings. She's playing games to get under our skin and make us react.

But I won't give her the satisfaction.

"Can we help you with something?" Sarah asks, her voice tense.

Emily leans in close, her breath hot against my ear. "I hear you and Jack have a little secret baby on the way. How scandalous."

My heart races as her words sink in. How could she know about that? I thought we had kept it a secret.

But before I can react, Sarah stands up, her expression livid.

"That's enough, Emily. You have no right to talk about Olivia's personal life like that," she says, her voice shaking with anger.

Emily smirks, her eyes glittering with malice. "Oh, come on. It's just a joke. Can't you take a little ribbing?"

But I know that there's nothing funny about what she's saying. She's trying to hurt us and make us feel small and insignificant.

And as Emily walks away, her laughter ringing in our ears, I can feel a sense of anger and disgust rising in my chest. I won't let her win. I won't let her manipulate or control me. I'll stay true to myself and to those I care about, no matter what.

Sarah and I sit silently, both seething with anger and frustration. Emily's words have hit a nerve, and we both feel vulnerable and exposed.

Finally, Sarah breaks the silence. "I can't stand that woman. She's so cruel and manipulative."

I nod in agreement, my voice shaking with emotion. "I know. It's like Emily gets pleasure out of hurting people."

Sarah takes a deep breath, trying to steady her nerves. "We need to be careful around her. She's not someone we can trust."

I know that Sarah is right. Emily is a dangerous player in this game, and we need to be vigilant to protect ourselves and those we care about.

"I'll talk to Jack," I say, my voice determined. "We need to ensure he knows what's going on."

Sarah nods. "Good idea. And in the meantime, we need to stick together and stay strong. We can't let her get the best of us."

"Thank you. You're a devoted friend," I say. I know with her help I can face whatever comes my way, no matter how difficult or painful.

As we finish our meal and make our way out of the restaurant, I can feel Emily's eyes on me, watching and waiting for me to react. I know that Emily is a horrible person. But I won't let her win. No one will ever trample anything I hold dear.

As Sarah and I stand in the parking lot, there is a rumble of thunder in the distance. It gets windy. I can already feel the humid air before the storm. I stand in the wind looking through the window of the restaurant. I see Emily shaking her head and laughing with Daniel.

Emily is a poisonous snake that hides on the side of the road I must pass. But I will beat her down.

Chapter 14. Jack

I know Olivia has returned to the studio. I haven't gotten a chance to see her. When I walk into a restaurant to meet Jeff, the banker, I know Olivia is sharing her dinner with Sarah on the other side of the city.

The restaurant where Jeff and I dine is exquisitely decorated with plush velvet chairs and elegant chandeliers casting a warm glow over the dining room. Beautiful artwork lines the walls, and the soft murmur of conversation creates a soothing background hum.

As we settle into our seats, the waiter approaches us with menus. We settle on grilled lamb chops, truffle risotto, and a bottle of vintage Cabernet.

As we dine, Jeff and I discuss his investment ideas for the studio.

Jeff is a smart man in his mid-sixties. His bald head and glasses reflect under the light. He can remember the restaurant food menu with a glance.

He speaks thoughtfully and with a deep understanding of the industry, sharing his insights and suggestions for how we can maximize our profits and grow the business.

I listen intently, before saying, "Jeff, I like the way you present yourself. You're sharp and insightful."

Jeff smiles a little. "I like your deep passion for the film industry, unlimited capacity for creation, and unbreakable will." I feel Jeff and I could be good business partners eventually. I need to push a little.

"You see, Jeff, the film industry is in a state of flux right now," I say, my tone confident and positive. "But with the right investments and the right team, we can capitalize on this change and take the studio to new heights."

Jeff listens attentively, nodding his head in agreement. "I see what you're saying," he says, his tone thoughtful. "But what sets your studio apart from the rest? Why should I invest in you?"

I lean forward, feeling a surge of excitement building within me. "Because we have the best team in the business," I say, my voice strong and assertive. "We're smart, we're passionate, and we know how to get things done." I take a sip of wine and begin to describe the profits we've been making each year. "Jeff, let me tell you about our profit margins," I say, my tone confident and assured. "Over the past few years, we've seen consistent growth in our earnings, and we're projected to continue that trend in the years to come."

Jeff listens closely, his eyes fixed on me as I continue to speak. "Last year alone, we saw a 15% increase in profits, and we're on track to exceed that number this year. With your investment, we could see even greater growth and success."

Jeff nods his head in approval. "That's quite impressive," he says, his tone serious. "I can see that you know what you're doing."

I nod proudly, "Yes, we do. And with your support, we could take this studio to new heights."

"I like what I'm hearing," Jeff says, a small smile playing at the corners of his mouth. "And I believe in your capability to make this happen."

I grin. Jeff's words make me feel satisfied. Jeff's belief in my vision is a significant step forward for the studio, and I'm excited to see where this new partnership will take us.

As the night wears on, we enjoy the delicious food and wine, savoring each bite and sip. The waiter politely removes used plates without a minute's delay, and the service is impeccable, with the waitstaff attending to our every need with quiet efficiency.

By the time we shake hands goodbye, Jeff tells me he wants to be my long-term investor. Great!

This is another wonderful evening. I'm so happy. I need to share this good news with Olivia. On my way home, I call Olivia, but I can't reach her. She must be having fun with her best friend Sarah.

As I sit at my desk in my study, poring over a proposal, my phone rings. I pick it up to hear Olivia's voice at the other end.

"Hey, Olivia, I'm so glad to hear from you. I know you returned to the studio, and I wanted to hear your cute voice," I say, my voice gruff.

"Jack, sorry, I had dinner in an Italian restaurant with Sarah. The noise was much louder than my ring tone. You sound tired."

"Where are you? Are you driving in this storm?" I look out through the window at the lightning, starting to worry about her. I know she doesn't like to drive in the dark, and driving in the stormy night could be harder.

Olivia's voice is shaky as she speaks. "Yes, and I'm really scared."

"Olivia, find a place to park, lock your car door, and tell me where you are. I'll pick you up." I stand up and get ready to leave.

"No, Jack. It has nothing to do with driving in the storm. It's Emily. Emily threatened me in the restaurant tonight, and I don't know what she will do next."

Emily is not to be underestimated; my heart races as I hear her words.

"Are you okay?" I ask, my voice reassuring.

"I'm okay. Sarah told me what Emily tried to do to you. Now Emily's after me, and she may set a trap for me too."

I can hear the worry in her voice, and it makes my blood boil. How dare Emily threaten Olivia like that? She's gone too far.

"Don't worry. I'll take care of this," I say, my voice low and menacing.

Olivia sounds relieved. "Thank you. I miss you so much."

My heart aches as I hear her words. I miss her too, more than words can express.

"I'll get you. Just tell me where you are," I say, my voice filled with determination.

As soon as I get the address, I rush out of my study and head to my car, driving as fast as I can through the storm. As I pull up to the address that Olivia gave me, I can see her car parked in front, and I know that the girl I love is inside, waiting for me.

I take a deep breath and step out of my car, making my way to the front door. When I knock, Olivia opens it, her eyes filled with relief.

"I'm so glad you're here," she says, her voice trembling.

I wrap my arms around her, holding her close. "I'm here. I couldn't wait till tomorrow to see you."

Olivia looks up at me, her eyes shining with tears. "I don't know what I would do without you."

I don't want to send Olivia to her apartment; instead, I drive her to mine. It's the first time Olivia has walked into my home.

As the storm rages outside, we sit together on the couch, holding each other close, and Olivia tells me more about what happened at the restaurant.

"Jack, I can tell Emily is trying to get to Daniel, and you should be ready for it," Olivia says quietly, leaning on my shoulder.

"I'm ready for anything," I say.

"They may team up to damage you." Olivia puts her hand on mine.

I kiss her. I hate intrigue, but I have no fear of adversaries.

"I'll talk to Daniel," I say, my voice deep and authoritative. "He needs to know what kind of person Emily really is."

"And I'll stay out of her way. I don't want to give her any more chances to hurt me," Olivia says with a confident smile. This is my brave girl. I sigh deeply inside.

I hold her close. The feeling of protectiveness fully occupies me. I won't let anyone hurt Olivia, not now, not ever.

"I can fix this," I say, my voice firm.

Olivia nods, her eyes filled with determination. "Together."

I stand up. "Olivia, we haven't spent time together for a while. Let's not waste it on that snake of a woman. Let's have some fun." I turn on the music and bring a glass of water to Olivia.

We sip water and begin discussing her spy movie. Her eyes are shining, and her cheeks turn red. She looks so cute and glows in the dim lighting. As Olivia and I continue our conversation, we dive deeper into the details of her spy role on set. Olivia becomes animated, gesturing wildly as she describes the action-packed scenes she's been filming since I've been gone.

"I get to do all sorts of cool stuff," she says, a gleeful look in her eye. "I get to jump out of helicopters, fight off a traitor, and save the day."

I laugh, amused. "You're a regular James Bond, aren't you?"

Olivia grins, tossing her hair back. "Oh, you have no idea. I'm like the female version of 007."

We chat for a while longer. At one point Olivia describes a particularly difficult scene she had to film, where she had to run through a crowded market while chased by enemy soldiers.

"I felt like a complete idiot," she says, shaking her head. "I was running like a chicken with its head cut off."

I can't help but laugh at the mental image. "I'm sure it wasn't that bad."

Olivia grins, rolling her eyes. "Oh, trust me. It was bad."

As we're joking and laughing, the thunder outside fades. The night wears on. I lead her into my bedroom. "Olivia, you need a good rest."

Olivia looks around the room with appreciation. "I love this place. It's so elegant and refined."

I smile. "It's not my creation. I do have a good interior designer, though."

Olivia says, "This room is stylish and comfortable."

I pick her up and put her on my bed carefully. "The best place is the bed." I find her a beautiful silk nightgown from the closet. She tosses it back to me when I hand it to her.

"I don't want someone else's clothes. I want your shirt."

I show her the price tag. "Hey, cheapskate, this is for you." Olivia carefully checks the size and the feel of the cloth and smiles happily.

I kiss her and say, "Good night." Then I turn away.

"Where are you going?" she asks me. Her face shows confusion.

"Guest room," I reply.

"Why?"

"I don't want to hurt you or our baby." I smile at her and close the bedroom door.

I stand in the hall.

I am shocked by my own words. "Our baby."

The king-size bed in the guestroom is wonderfully comfortable. I'm that kind of person. Whenever my head touches the pillow, I can fall asleep. Soon, I feel drowsy. Just when I'm about to fall asleep, the guest room door opens quietly, and Olivia crawls onto the bed and hugs me.

"Sorry, Jack, tonight I want to be with you," she says. I can feel her warm breath.

I know I'm in trouble now.

It's so hard for me to walk away from her. Now, she's on my bed. A little sheep comes to visit a hungry wolf.

"Thank you, Jack." Her voice is low.

"For what?" I ask. I put my hands under my head to avoid touching her soft body.

"You said 'our baby.' It's the first time you've said so."

"Olivia," I call her in the dark.

"What?" she asks.

"Please do me a favor. Will you?"

"Sure. What do you want?"

"Go back to your room," I say sternly.

"No, why?" Olivia shakes her head, and her hair brushes my face.

"I have a critical meeting tomorrow. I need rest."

Olivia does not reply, but I can feel her fingers pinch my chest.

"Stop. I'm dangerous," I say. "I can't control myself. You should know better." I start to lose my patience. I turn to my side, show my back to her.

"Jack." I hear Olivia calling me.

"What now?"

"I want to tell you a secret." From her voice, I know she must feel shy about what she is going to tell me.

"Go on. I'm listening."

"I love you."

"I know that."

"I've loved you since I was eleven years old." Her voice sounds excited, and relieved that she has finally spoken her little secret.

I turn back and look at her. I can't believe what I just heard.

"Do you remember how many times you turned me down?"

"No."

"I can share some with you now. It was the first day of spring break, you and Paul wanted to go rock climbing. I wanted to join you. Paul said yes, but you said no."

"No, I cannot remember it." I try to recall the memory, but I can't remember it. I feel Olivia's hand touching my hair gently.

"You said, 'this is not a game for little girls.' You've been bossy since you were a teenager." Olivia smiles. "That day, before you left, I gave you a Lindt Lindor Truffle Chocolate, and I still have the red wrapping." Her eyes are shining in the dark.

I feel so bad. I can't remember any of this. But I can remember her little pink cheeks when she was a child.

"You were like Paul's tail, aways following him around." I finally remember something about the old days.

"No, you're wrong. I was following *you*, not Paul. You were smart enough to find out if you wanted to, but you never paid attention to me."

"How could I know that? You were so tiny back then." I smile, kissing her hands.

"I jumped a lot, I wanted to grow up taller and quicker, so you would notice me. I had been waiting for ten years, until we had that one-night stand on Paul's wedding day."

I feel my heart melting.

"Olivia, do you remember what you said to me that steamy night we shared in the park?" I look into her eyes, then I repeat her words, "You said, 'you are the first male to touch my body, and I hope you will be the last one." I hug her gently. "Olivia, let me be your man." I hug her. I can feel her heartbeat.

In the dark, I ask myself: Has Olivia already broken all my rules?

Chapter 15. Olivia

The following day I awake to the sounds of Jack bringing me breakfast in bed. He's wearing a white shirt and carrying a tray of food in his hands, like a waiter bringing food to the table. He looks so kind and gentle, with all the bossiness from work gone from his face and demeanor.

As he sets the tray beside me, I can feel his love radiating from every word and move. I smile up at him, feeling my heart overflow with joy.

The summer morning sun shines brightly through the window, casting a warm glow over the beautiful landscape outside. It's the perfect backdrop for our moment of happiness together.

This is the life I have been dreaming of for many years.

"Good morning, my love," Jack says, his voice soft and sweet. "I wanted to make this morning special for you."

Warmth spreads through me, Jack cares for me so profoundly. "Thank you, Jack," I say, my voice filled with gratitude. "This is so lovely."

As we enjoy our breakfast together, I feel our love growing stronger with each passing moment, and I know that we're meant to be together.

"This is for our baby," Jack says, putting one of his baking eggs into my plate.

Our baby. It's the second time he has said so.

As we finish our meal, I cuddle beside Jack, feeling his warmth and love envelop me. I look up at his handsome face next to mine. I can't help but wish that we could spend the entire day together. But alas, duty calls, and Jack has a meeting to attend.

"I don't want to go to work today," I say, pouting slightly as I lean into his shoulder.

Jack chuckles softly, his eyes crinkling with amusement. "I know, my love, but we have responsibilities. And besides, we'll have plenty of time to spend together later." Jack starts cleaning up.

"How long is your plenty of time?" I ask, holding my breath.

"As long as I can breathe." Jack places the tray on the end table and looks into my eyes when he says so.

"What about all your rules?" I cannot believe my ears.

"Gone." Jack stares at me. His gaze is soft, but his voice is firm.

"Jack." I run to him and throw myself into his arms.

"I could not sleep last night. Those rules are all gone, forever," he says, his voice very deep but gentle.

I cry and laugh at the same time. I cannot stop my tears.

Jack kisses me, saying, "We need to get ready to work. I have a meeting at 10:00 a.m."

"Okay," I sigh softly.

I know he's right, but I still can't help but feel a sense of reluctance as we dress and head out to Jack's car.

As we pull up to the parking lot, Jack drops me off to pick up my car. He takes my hand in his. "I wish we could spend more time together," I say, my voice soft and wistful.

"I know, my love, but I promise we'll make time for each other," Jack replies, his tone filled with sincerity.

I watch as he heads off to his meeting. I feel a little movement inside of me. It is the first kick my baby gives to me.

I drive away. On this beautiful day, life is so wonderful.

I'm not in any shots this morning, so I go shopping. I love shopping and am eager to find the perfect gifts for my brother's baby girl and my future son.

The shopping center is bustling with activity. The colorful displays and cheerful music put me in a good mood, and I can't help but smile as I make my way from store to store.

What should I buy for my future niece? I get lost in all the colorful clothes. Jane would know better. I dial Jane's number and wait eagerly for her to answer. After a few rings, she picks up and greets me with a cheerful hello.

"Hey, Jane, how are you doing?" I ask.

"I'm good, thanks for asking. How about you?" she responds.

"I'm doing well, thanks. Listen, I'm out shopping and want to pick up something for my baby niece. Do you have any ideas or suggestions for what I should get?" I ask.

Jane laughs and says, "Well, we've been looking for a pink bed set for the baby's bed. It would be perfect for the nursery."

"That's a great idea! I'll keep an eye out for something like that. It sounds so cute," I reply.

I want to ask Jane what I should buy for my baby boy, but I stop. My brother, Paul, and his wife, Jane, know nothing about the relationship between Jack and me.

I should talk to Paul first.

After finishing the conversation with Jane, I start to browse through the baby section. I pick out some adorable onesies and little hats, imagining what it will be like to hold my little one in my arms. I can't help but get excited about having my own baby boy one day.

I make a mental note to start planning for his nursery, imagining the perfect color scheme and decorations to create a cozy and welcoming space for him to grow and thrive. I like light blue, but what color would Jack like? I need to ask him.

A wrist sporting a sparkling crystal bracelet reaches for the same light blue baby dress I do. This bracelet looks familiar, and I can't help but shudder. I turn around and see that it is Emily. Beside her stands a big man in black sportswear who looks like a boxer. Emily looks at me without saying a word, eyes full of jealousy and hatred. The rugged man stands expressionless beside her, but I know that if Emily wants to hurt me, he could act at any time.

I leave. I try my best to stay calm. I'm carrying Jack's baby. I can't give Emily any opportunity to hurt my baby.

I decide to shake off Emily and the strange man and make my way out of the shopping center. I walk through the bright and bustling mall and head to the elevator. But as I turn a corner, my heart sinks. I see Emily and the tall and intimidating-looking man have cut ahead of me. My mood suddenly changes, and I feel foreboding.

It is not a coincidence I met Emily in the shopping center. Emily is following me.

I want to call Jack, but I know Jack is in an important meeting. So, I take a seat inside the food court. There are a lot of people around. I should be safe here. I call Sarah.

I dial Sarah's number and wait anxiously for her to answer. After a few rings, she picks up and greets me with a hello.

"Sarah, it's Olivia. Listen, I'm out shopping. Emily and a big guy are following me," I say in a panicked voice.

"What?! Where are you?" Sarah asks urgently.

"I'm at the food court inside the mall."

"Which mall?"

"Next to the Italian restaurant we were at recently. They followed me here," I reply, my heart racing.

"Okay, stay calm. Try to keep a distance from Emily and the guy, and head towards the security office on the first floor near Macy's. I'll call Jack and let him know what's going on," Sarah instructs.

"Sarah, Jack is in an important meeting—"

"I must call Jack; I don't care what the meeting is about. Call 9-1-1 if you feel you're in danger."

Sarah hangs up. I know she must call Jack now. I stand up and head to the security office. I start walking quickly, trying to lose Emily and the big guy. But they keep getting closer and closer. I hear their footsteps behind me, and I feel even more scared. I call Sarah again.

"Sarah, they're getting closer. What do I do?!" I whisper into the phone.

"Just keep moving towards the security office. Jack is on his way there now. He'll be able to help you," Sarah reassures me.

I hear an incoming call; it's Jack.

"Olivia, I'll be there soon. I will not allow anyone to hurt you." Jack's voice is very calm and firm.

"Jack, thank you, I feel much better now." I see the security office up ahead. I run towards it, hoping I can make it there before Emily and the big guy catch up.

"Jack, I'm there. I see the security office," I say, trying to catch my breath.

"Okay, good. Stay inside," Jack says.

I make it to the security office just as Emily and the big guy catch up to me. I quickly duck inside and lock the door. Then I feel I'm safe.

I report to the security guy that they have been following me, then call Sarah. "Sarah, I made it. Thank you so much for your help," I say, tears streaming down my face.

"It's okay, Olivia. Just stay inside and wait for Jack," Sarah says, trying to calm me down.

The security guy tells me Emily and the guy are gone. I feel grateful for Sarah's quick thinking and support. And as I see Jack's familiar face through the window of the security office, I know that everything will be okay.

As Jack enters the security office, I feel relief.

"Thanks for coming, Jack," I say, grateful for his presence.

"I'm sorry that you've gone through this. Are you sure you're okay?" he asks, placing his hand on my shoulder.

I nod my head again, feeling comforted by his touch.

Jack approaches the security guy and says, "I need you to check the security footage from earlier today. Emily and a big guy followed Olivia to the shopping center, and we check the security cameras."

The security guy nods and starts pulling up the footage on the computer screen. As we watch, I can feel my heart pounding, wondering what we might see.

Suddenly, Jack shouts, "There they are! That's them, right there!" He points to the screen, where we can see Emily and the big guy following me through the shopping center.

Without hesitation, Jack pulls out his phone and dials the police. "We need to file a report right away. Two people followed my girlfriend and threatened her. We have evidence on the security footage."

The tension in the room is palpable as we wait for the police to arrive.

Soon, two policemen show up in the security office. Jack speaks to them in a firm and urgent tone, giving them all the information they need to take action.

As they file the report, Jack turns to me and says, "Don't worry, we're going to make sure they can never hurt you again. We'll see this through to the end."

I nod, grateful for Jack's support and strength in the face of danger. And when he gets the confirmation number for the police report, I know we're one step closer to putting this whole ordeal behind us.

When I return to the studio, it is lunchtime. I'm suddenly starving. It happens more often now since my baby is growing.

The moment I walk into the dining hall, something is wrong, but I can't find what it could be. I can feel the tension in the air. Everyone is watching me, waiting for me to do something wrong or dislike me.

I grab my food and try to find a table to sit down. As I sit down to eat, three actresses stand up and move to another table. All the tables are full now except mine.

I try to ignore it and focus on my food, but it's hard.

Then I see those three actresses whispering to each other and then looking in my direction. I can feel my cheeks turning red with embarrassment. I'm frustrated and angry.

Just then, Sarah comes over to me with a look of regret.

"I'm so sorry, Olivia," she says.

"Don't say that." I force a smile. I don't want to upset Sarah.

"I think I might have accidentally let something slip to Emily about your situation with Jack."

I can feel my heart sinking as I realize what she's saying. "What did you tell her?" I ask, my voice shaking.

Sarah shakes her head hard. "I didn't tell her anything. She must've overheard something." Sarah hesitates momentarily, then says, "I might have mentioned the baby, and I wanted Jack to take responsibility for it."

I feel my face turning red with anger. "How could you do that?" I hiss. "Now Emily is using it against me to destroy my career."

Sarah looks apologetic. "I'm sorry, I didn't realize Emily was listening," she says.

I take a deep breath and try to compose myself. "It's not your fault," I say. "But we need to find a way to fix this."

As we talk, I can feel the eyes of the other people in the dining hall still on me, then I hear the words "secret baby." I feel a wave of rage washing over me. I want to stand up and tell them I'm no longer carrying a secret baby. And I earned the lead role through my effort and demanding work.

But I decide to keep quiet.

I need to give Jack more time. Let Jack announce I'm his fiancée first.

I look at Sarah. She seems angry and sad. "Sarah," I call her.

"What?" Sarah raises her head and gazes at me.

"Please, don't feel bad. You were trying to help me. You are my best friend. Thank you," I say sincerely. I remember how much support she offered when Emily was following me.

"You helped me a lot in the mall today." I smile.

"Olivia, who is the big guy?" Sarah looks nervous.

"I don't know. I've never seen him before. He's a big, tall guy, but he moves faster than ordinary people. He could be a boxer or private bodyguard."

"Sounds like a hitman," Sarah says.

I recall the incident in the mall and try to describe that guy as much as possible. "His eyes are cold, and his face is motionless. When he walks, his arms and body do not move much, only his legs, and he takes long strides."

"He may have unique skills or a military background. Don't you think so?" Sarah looks at my face.

"I wish I knew more."

Suddenly, I have a horrible feeling. Is this another trap Emily set for Jack? Can she use me to get at Jack?

Chapter 16. Jack

In the dim light, the nightclub is full of people. The sound of techno music and the chatter and laughter of other patrons are so loud. The lights constantly change, casting unusual colors on the excited faces of the crowd and the modern art sculptures on the wall. Eye-catching bottles of wine line the bars as if declaring that this is a place for drunkards.

Alex invites me and a few other directors to have fun here after all the complex work we've been doing. As I sit with Alex and James, we discuss the ongoing films and share our opinions on each other's work. I take a sip of my drink, then receive a call from Olivia.

"Excuse me." I nod to my friends, stand up, and walk away from the table.

"Hi, Jack. Can you talk?" she asks, sounding a little nervous.

"Sure, go on," I reply.

"I want to tell you what happened in the dining hall during lunchtime."

After hearing the story, I tell Olivia, "Nothing to be surprised about. Nothing needs to be worried about. It will be all over soon."

Olivia sounds relieved, "Thank you, Jack. I'm better now that I've talked to you."

I say, "Olivia, I think it's time we let your brother Paul know about us. I want to marry you and spend the rest of my life with you."

Olivia's voice becomes extremely excited. "Really? You mean it?"

"Yes, I do. I can't keep our love a secret forever. It's time we let the people we care about know about our relationship." The bar is very noisy, and I must yell on the phone. After I tell Olivia my decision, I feel much better. It's a big relief.

Olivia sounds cheerful, saying, "Jack, I'm so happy to hear your words. But how should we tell Paul?"

"Paul's birthday is next weekend. Let's do it then. It will be a great surprise for him. And we can tell him and Jane about our baby too." I already have a plan in my mind.

Olivia says happily, "I like it. That sounds like a great idea. I can't wait to see their reaction."

A drunk man hits my shoulder when he passes. He tries several times but still can't open the exit door. I tell Olivia, "I can't wait to see your smile that day." At the same time, I help the man open the door.

"You always know how to make me happy, Jack." Olivia still wants to talk, but the drunk man needs more help.

"That's because I love you more than anything in this world. Olivia, I must go." I hang up the call and head after the drunk man.

"Excuse me, sir," I say, catching him in the parking lot outside the nightclub.

The man ignores my words. His hands are trembling. He can't get the car key from his pocket.

"Hey, buddy, you've had too much to drink. It's not safe for you to drive."

"Mind your own business. I'm fine!" His voice is angry.

"No, you're not fine. You're swaying and stumbling all over the place. You could get hurt or hurt someone else." I stand there blocking his car door.

The drunk man rolls his eyes: "Who do you think you are? Mind your own business!"

I stand still. "I mind my own business. My business is making sure that everyone is safe."

"Are you a policeman?" The voice is low the first time. I realize he still can think well.

I smile. "I'm a policeman under cover," I reply. "Now, let me call a taxi for you."

The drunk man raises his voice again. "No, I don't need a taxi. I can drive myself!" He pushes me away. He is a strong man.

I call Jay, my assistant, "Jay, get out here. Parking lot. Quick."

Soon I see Jay run out of the nightclub. "What's up?"

"Call a taxi, send this gentleman home, and ensure he gets inside okay."

"Yes, boss." Jay nods, then calls a taxi.

The drunk man finally gives up. "Fine, call your damn taxi."

Jay is talking on the phone, then turns to me, "Got it, boss. Taxi will be here in five minutes."

I look at the angry man. "Okay, my assistant Jay will take you home. Just wait here, and he'll take care of everything."

The drunk man shows me a stone face. "Whatever, man. Just leave me alone."

I smile at that man. "Some people just don't appreciate a good deed. But you make me feel better. I finally found a man who can be grumpier than me." Then I walk back to the nightclub.

The next weekend, as we planned, Olivia and I attend Paul's birthday party. The sun is shining brightly in the blue sky as we arrive at Paul's backyard for the festivities. The landscape is breathtaking, with green grass, tall trees, and blooming flowers surrounding us. A pool is on one side of the yard, and a large outdoor bar is on the other.

As I walk through the crowd, I see many of Paul's wealthy business associates dressed in their finest. The attendants are busy serving drinks and appetizers, ensuring each guest is tended.

In one corner of the yard is a group of people playing lawn games, while in another, a DJ is playing music for those who want to dance.

The atmosphere is lively and energetic. As I walk around, I notice a lot of people discussing business. I fully understand: these smart people always take advantage of their opportunities for future business.

"Where is Paul?" Olivia searches for her brother. She's eager to share our good news with him.

"It's more crowded than the flea market here. Let's search for Paul." I hold Olivia's hand and keep looking.

In the center of the backyard is a large fountain with water flowing gently. I see Paul holding a glass of wine and greeting the guests, surrounded by friends. His wife Jane is beside him, and I can see the happiness on their faces.

"Look, they're near the fountain." I point out Paul to Olivia. Then, I take a deep breath and we make our way over to him.

As I walk through the crowd at Paul's birthday party, I can feel the tension building inside me. I've been looking forward to this moment for so long, but now that I'm here, I feel a knot in my stomach.

"Hey, Paul! Happy birthday, man! I've got a present for you," I say, holding out a small, wrapped box.

Paul hears my voice, and he turns. His smile goes away when he sees that I'm holding Olivia's hand.

Paul looks at me skeptically, "What is it?"

"You'll have to open it to find out," I say, grinning.

Paul unwraps the box and pulls out a fancy watch. He looks impressed and grateful, but I can tell something is still bothering him.

"So, Jack, what's going on? Why are you here together?" Paul asks, his tone turning serious.

I take a deep breath, feeling my heart pounding in my chest. "Paul, I have something to tell you. I want to marry your sister, Olivia."

Paul does not reply. I can tell he is trying hard to calm down.

"Excuse us," he says politely to the friends surrounding him. Then he pulls me away. Olivia wants to follow us; Paul lifts his hand and stops her.

I glance at Olivia's face; her face is pale white. She stands there, not sure what to do. She must feel very embarrassed in front of his brother's friends. I smile at her, trying to make her feel a little better.

I follow Paul inside. Along the way, many people say hi to Paul. Paul smiles at them politely but without stopping.

Paul leads me to his study. He closes the door tightly. Then he turns to me.

Paul's face goes blank, and for a moment, there is complete silence between us. Finally, he says, "Jack, I can't let you do that."

"What? Why not?" I ask, my tone growing defensive.

"Because you're a playboy, Jack. I've seen how you treat women, and I won't let my sister be another one of your conquests," Paul says firmly.

I feel a sudden surge of anger and frustration. "Paul, you don't understand. I love Olivia. I want to spend the rest of my life with her. I've changed, Paul. I'm not the same guy I used to be."

Paul shakes his head. "I'm sorry, Jack. Our parents both passed away in a car accident. I'm the one who must protect Olivia. I can't approve of this. You need to prove to me that you're serious about my sister. You must show me you're committed to making this work."

I feel my jaw clenching, and I know I'm on the verge of losing my cool. "Paul, you have no idea how committed I am. I love Olivia more than anything, and I'll do anything to make her happy."

Paul looks at me skeptically. "Anything?"

"Yes, anything," I reply.

"Okay then, prove it. Show me that you're willing to do whatever it takes to make this work," Paul says, his tone still firm.

I take a deep breath, feeling my anger dissipate slightly. "What do you want me to do?"

Paul looks at me seriously. "First, you need to stop seeing other women. You must prove to me that you're willing to be faithful to my sister."

"I'm already faithful to Olivia. I haven't been with anyone else since I met her on your wedding day," I say, slightly defensive.

"Well, you need to prove it to me," Paul says firmly.

"Okay, what else?" I ask, feeling slightly defeated.

"You need to start treating Olivia with the respect she deserves. It would be best to show her you're serious about this relationship," Paul says.

"I already treat Olivia with respect," I reply, feeling my frustration building again.

"Really? It would be best if you started putting her first," Paul says.

"I do." My voice is firm.

"Jack, we are best friends. That's the brotherhood. We can do business together because we have the same mindset on work. But on family life, we are different. I'm a family man; you are not. Olivia needs a happy family life. I don't think you can give it to her."

"So?" I ask, holding my breath.

"So..." Paul takes a deep breath. "I cannot approve of it. It's the end."

I feel guilty in my chest, Paul is right. I haven't been the best boyfriend to Olivia. I've been so focused on my career and my needs that I haven't given her the attention and love she deserves.

"You're right, Paul." I take a deep breath and try to remain calm. "I understand your concern, but I love your sister. I have changed and am ready to commit to her for life."

Paul looks at me skeptically. "How can I trust that you won't hurt her? You have a reputation for playing around with women."

"I admit that I've made mistakes in the past, but Olivia is different. She has changed me, and I am a better man because of her," I say sincerely.

Paul crosses his arms. "I need to talk to Olivia about it."

"I understand," I reply.

We end the conversation. When I leave Paul's study, I see Olivia waiting for me in the living room. Paul sees his sister too. He stops, and seems to want to talk to her, but then strides out, leaving Olivia and me inside.

"How did that go?" Olivia runs to me.

"Not approved. Paul does not trust me," I say.

"Jack, we don't need his approval." Olivia looks up at me, her voice firm.

"Listen, Olivia. You're a lucky girl. You have the best brother in the world. We don't need his approval, but a little patience will bring us a long, happy life, not just you and me, but also with Paul and Jane."

"You're right." Olivia sighs.

We walk out together, but I don't hold Olivia's hand in front of Paul and Jane.

The rest of the party passes in an awkward silence between Paul and me. I can't help but feel disappointed and frustrated, but I know this decision cannot be rushed. I must be patient and hope that Paul will eventually come around.

I sit in the corner of the yard, feeling like I don't belong there. I can see Paul talking to some businessman friends, laughing, and drinking. But I can also feel his disapproving eyes on me. I've become a target of his judgment, and I can't shake off this uneasy feeling.

Suddenly, I feel a presence beside me. It's Olivia. She sits down next to me, looking worried. She's been quiet for a long time, ever since Paul voiced his objections to our marriage.

I turn to her, gazing into her beautiful eyes. "I love you, Olivia. Paul will agree because he'll see our true love."

Olivia's face lights up with a smile. We sit together waiting for the party to be over. The time becomes prolonged.

Someone touches my shoulder. I look up. It's the drunk man I met in the nightclub a few days ago.

"Hey, Jack, I'm William." I'm surprised. I didn't expect to ever see him again, especially in this situation. However, I put on a smile and greet him.

"Hello, William. It's nice to see you again."

"I'm feeling great, thanks to you," he says with a grin. "Thank you for taking care of me the other night. I could have been in big trouble if it weren't for you."

"No problem." I don't want to talk about it.

William smiles at me. "Your assistant left me his business card, so I know who you are. I've heard a lot about you lately. You're quite the hotshot in the film industry, aren't you?"

"I have a passion for making the best movies," I reply.

"Well, I think you're doing a damn good job," he says, sipping his drink. "And I'm not just saying that because I'm a big investor in LA."

I raise an eyebrow in surprise. "You're an investor? That's interesting. What kind of projects are you involved in?"

William leans in and lowers his voice. "Well, I can't give away all my secrets, can I? But let's just say I have my hands in many different pies. And I'm always looking for new opportunities to invest in."

"That's quite impressive. It must be exciting to have that kind of power and influence." I smile.

William chuckles. "Well, it has its perks, that's for sure. But it's not all sunshine and rainbows, you know. There's a lot of pressure to make the right decisions and turn a profit. It can be a stressful business." He pauses, then laughs. "It also can turn me into a drunk."

"I can imagine," I say, sipping my drink. "But it sounds like you have a good handle on things."

William smiles. "I like to think so. But enough about me. I'm more interested in hearing about you. I've heard some interesting things, you know. Rumors about your personal life, your relationships with some of the...."

I see Olivia's face turn red. I interrupt him calmly, "Look, William, my personal life is my own, and I'd appreciate it if you didn't pry into it."

William holds up his hands in a gesture of surrender. "Okay, okay. I get it. I didn't mean to pry. I just thought we were having a friendly conversation." Then he turns to Olivia. "Who is this lovely young lady?" he asks.

"My fiancée, Olivia," I say.

"I'm Paul's sister." Olivia looks at William and smiles a little.

"I see." William nods and smiles meaningfully. "Olivia, what a beautiful name, just like its owner. It's wonderful."

"Olivia is the best girl I've ever met," I praise sincerely. This is the first time I've complimented Olivia in front of others, and my words make her blush again, but this time with happy shyness.

William grins, happy to say, "Jack and Olivia, I wish you all the best. Jack, we'll meet again. Goodbye." He raises his glass to me and leaves.

"He's a nice man," Olivia says, watching William's back.

But I catch some unpleasant information in his meaningful smile.

When the party is finally over, Olivia and I are both tired, and now, my best friend has become an obstacle to my happiness.

Chapter 17. Olivia

We drive back to Jack's home directly after we leave Paul's birthday party. The conversation between Jack and Paul at the party still weighs heavily on our minds. As we walk through the door, I can't help but feel a sense of unease. Jack senses my apprehension and wraps an arm around me, pulling me close to him.

"Hey, don't worry about it," he says. "We'll figure it out. I won't let Paul's disapproval get in the way of us being together."

I nod, taking a deep breath to calm my nerves. "I know, but it's hard not to think about it."

Jack leads me to the living room, where we sit on the couch, looking at the beautiful view. The sky is painted in shades of pink and orange, with the sun setting behind the buildings in the distance. It's a serene scene, but I can't help feeling the tension between us.

"Let's not think about Paul for now," Jack says, breaking the silence. "We have shared an entire day together."

I smile, grateful for the change of subject. "Yeah, it's the first time we've stayed together for an entire day."

I lean on Jack's shoulder and start thinking about our baby. "Jack, Paul, and Jane want a light pink bed set for their baby girl. We should start planning for our baby boy too."

Jack's eyes light up. "What do you have in mind?"

"Light blue, like the clear sky in the fall." Then, I describe the nursery ideas of which I've been thinking.

Suddenly, Jack's phone rings, interrupting our conversation. He glances at the caller ID and frowns. "Sorry, this is Alex. I must take this," he says, getting up from the couch and walking to the other side of the room.

I sit on the couch, watching as he talks on the phone. I can tell from his tone that it's a work-related call. He speaks with a sense of urgency, his voice low and profound. I can only hear one name repeated a few times—*Jeff*.

As he hangs up the phone, he walks back over to me, his expression grim. "I have to go back to the studio," he says. "There's an issue with one of the films we're producing. I'm sorry. I know this isn't how we wanted to spend our evening."

"It's okay, Jack. I'll be fine here." I nod, understanding the demands of his job.

He leans down and gives me a quick kiss. "I won't be long. And when I get back, we'll talk more about our future family."

With that, he grabs his keys and heads out the door.

I'm left alone in Jack's home. The weight of Paul's disapproval still looms large, and now the absence of Jack only adds to it.

I shower, then rest on the bed, waiting for Jack's return. My phone vibrates. It's Paul.

"Is everything okay?" Paul asks.

"Yes, birthday boy."

"Hey, are you with Jack?" His voice is concerned.

"No, why?"

"I want to meet you tomorrow. Can you meet me at the Starbucks near the studio?"

I feel a knot in my stomach. I know this meeting will be unpleasant. "Sure, what time?"

"See you at eleven." Paul hangs up. At the same time, I hear the garage door opening. Jack is back.

"Jack, Paul just called," I tell him when he enters the master bedroom.

Jack walks over to the bed and sits down next to me. I can see the love and concern in him.

"What did he say?"

"He wants to meet me tomorrow at the Starbucks near the studio."

"What for?" Jack looks into my eyes.

"I don't know. But I have a feeling it's about us."

Jack takes my hand. "We'll face it together."

Jack turns off the light and goes to bed. He opens his arms and hugs me gently. Our bodies intertwine, and I feel calm. It is as if all my worries have melted away, replaced by the warmth and security of Jack's embrace. It's like we're two souls connected by an unbreakable bond. At that moment, I realize how much Jack means to me. It isn't just our passion, but how he makes me feel, and how he cares for the baby and me. He is more than just a lover; he is a partner, a friend, and a protector.

Next, I feel his hand slide gently over my pajamas and rest on my chest. Then, he deftly unbuttons my collar and slowly slides his hand into my pajamas. He gently touches my breasts, which have grown fuller with pregnancy. It is a very gentle touch. Then he kisses me from my forehead and moves down to my neck, chest, and entire body. We make love. It is a steamy, passionate encounter filled with love and tenderness. Jack is careful and gentle, ensuring he does not hurt the baby or me.

As we lay there, basking in the afterglow, Jack whispers, "I love you, Olivia. You and our baby mean everything to me."

Tears well up in my eyes as I look into his. "I love you too, Jack." I sigh. "I never want to lose you."

"You won't," he says, holding me close. "I'll always be here for you, no matter what."

At that moment, I know that I have found my soulmate.

As we drift off to sleep and wrap ourselves in each other's arms, I know tomorrow will be challenging since I need to meet Paul, my angry brother.

The next day I arrive at Starbucks early. I order a coffee and wait nervously for Paul. My brother comes in ten minutes later, looking stern.

"Hi, Paul," I say, trying to calm my voice.

"Hey," he responds coolly. We sit at a table, and Paul wastes no time getting to the point.

"I can't approve of you marrying Jack," he says bluntly.

"Why not?" I ask, trying to keep the frustration out of my voice.

"Because Jack is a playboy. I warned you before. I don't want my sister to be another notch on Jack's belt."

"I understand your concern, Paul, but I love Jack."

"Does Jack love you?"

"Yes. Paul, Jack loves me."

"Jack's love for women is like dewdrops, which disappear into the air at dawn." Paul shakes his head. "Your marriage would have no security."

"Paul, you and Jack are best friends. Do you think you really know Jack?" I feel a wave of disappointment washing over me.

"We grew up together," Paul replies very confidently.

"Paul, Jack is still growing. The way he treats me is quite different than if we were just dating. You are a perfect brother, and you are trying to protect me. You should be incredibly happy for me if you can see the truth."

"Olivia, I need to see the proof." Paul looks at me. His voice is firm.

"Okay, show me proof. How much do you love Jane?" I ask, staring into his eyes. Paul does not reply. "You can't. Only Jane knows how much you love her, right?" Paul looks at the coffee table and takes another sip of his coffee. I know what he's thinking. "We do not need your permission to get married, but Jack does not want to hurt you. Paul, I cannot wait for too long. I'm pregnant."

Paul raises his head, looking at me with surprise. "That is too bad." Paul bites his lip, looks away, and his face becomes incredibly nervous when he turns back.

"Olivia, there's something else I need to tell you," His expression one of concern.

"What is it?" I ask, my heart pounding in my chest.

Paul looks at me with concern in his eyes. "I've heard some rumors that Jack's involved in some shady business deals," he says. "And some people think he's not as honest as he seems."

I panic as I listen to Paul's words. I can't believe what he's saying. I've always known Jack to be a good, honest man.

"But where did you hear these rumors?" I ask, hoping to get more information.

Paul looks at me seriously. "At my birthday party, William, one of my investors, told me Jack lied to his friend Jeff, misleading Jeff to invest in the wrong project. "Paul looks me in the eyes. "You need to be careful, especially if you're planning on marrying him."

William. I think of that goofy guy with a glass of wine, and it's creepy to think of his smile at the time. I suddenly remember the scene where Jack left in a hurry after receiving a call yesterday evening. In that phone call, Jack seemed to repeatedly mention a man named Jeff. Jeff, who is this, Jeff? I felt confused listening to Paul's words. Could it be that Jack isn't who I thought he was?

"But I don't believe it," I say, my voice shaking with emotion. "Jack is a good man. He would never be involved in anything shady."

Paul looks at me with concern. "I hope you're right," he says. "But I just want to ensure you know what I've heard."

We sit silently for a few moments, both lost in our thoughts. Finally, I stand up from the table and say goodbye to Paul.

Walking away from Starbucks, my mind races with thoughts and doubts. Is it possible that Jack isn't the honest, good man I thought he was? Or is this just a rumor, a baseless accusation? I feel a mix of emotions—anger, confusion, and betrayal. I can't just sit around and do nothing, so I decide to take matters into my own hands and find out the truth. I need to learn more about Jack's past and business dealings. And I know that I need to confront him and ask him directly about these rumors.

At the studio parking lot, I meet Sarah. She's just gotten out of a van with a few others. She greets me with a big smile.

"Hey, Olivia, I have good news. I'm going to have a vital role in Alex's new movie. Our crew will go to France to shoot some scenes."

"Congratulations." I give Sarah a big hug.

Sarah quickly notices that something is wrong. "Olivia, what's wrong? You look pale. Is everything all right?" Sarah asks with concern.

I take a deep breath before answering her. "I just met my brother, Paul. He doesn't want me to marry Jack," I say, trying to keep my voice steady.

Sarah's eyes widen in surprise. "What? You got the monster to agree to marry you? Wow! I'm so happy for you!" Sarah jumps up and gives me a warm hug.

"Why are you not happy?" she asks.

"I told you. Paul disagrees."

"Why? They're friends, right?" Sarah asks.

"I don't want to talk about that," I reply. "Paul didn't say much, just that he doesn't think Jack is the right person for me."

Sarah looks thoughtful for a moment before speaking again. "Well, you know your brother. He's always been protective of you. He just needs some time to get used to the idea."

I nod in agreement but still can't shake off the feeling that something is wrong. "There's something else, Sarah," I say, my voice barely above a whisper.

"What is it?" she asks, her expression now serious.

"Jack may be cheating in his business dealings," I reply, looking down at the ground.

Sarah's eyes widen in shock. "What makes you think that?" she asks.

"I don't have any concrete evidence yet," I admit. "But Paul mentioned something to me, and I need to verify it secretly before I confront Jack."

Sarah nods understandingly. "I see," she says. "Well, let me know if there's anything I can do to help. You know I always have your back."

I smile gratefully at her. "Thanks, Sarah. I appreciate it."

As I walk into the studio, I can't help but feel a sense of unease. I know I need to learn the truth about Jack's business dealings, but I also don't want to lose him. I hope my suspicions are unfounded, but I can't shake off the feeling that there's more here than meets the eye.

I walk into the studio and knock on the director's door.

"Alex, I need to ask you something," I say as soon as I walk into his office.

"Of course. What's up?" he replies, looking up from his computer.

"I need to know what happened when you called Jack yesterday."

Alex sighs and rubs his forehead. "I hope you won't get involved in this mess, Olivia. But since you're here, I'll tell you what I know. I was working with a French movie company on a new film, and the proposal was approved. But then Jeff, the main investor, suddenly changed his mind and pulled out. We're left without funding and will have to cancel the project."

"Why would Jeff do that?" I ask, feeling even more confused.

"That's what we're all trying to figure out," Alex says, shaking his head. "Jack's been acting strange lately, and I feel he's involved in this somehow."

I can't believe what I'm hearing. Jack, my fiancé, the man I thought I knew so well, is allegedly involved in something deceitful and dishonest.

"What should we do now?" I ask, feeling a sense of panic rising in my chest.

"I think we need to confront Jack and get to the bottom of this," Alex says, determined.

I nod, feeling relieved that I'm not alone in this. "Okay, let's do it."

We make our way to Jack's office, and I can feel my heart racing with anticipation. I don't know what to expect, but I must find the truth. If Jack really did wrong, he needs to fix it. I can't marry a jerk.

We arrive at Jack's office. Jack's assistant, Jay, is working in the front room, and many file folders are open on his desk. I can tell he's dealing with problems.

Jay stands up and leads us into Jack's office politely. When we walk in, I see Jack standing near the window, looking out. His mind is outside somewhere.

"Jack, you have visitors," Jay says quietly. Jay knows Jack is close to me.

Jack turns to us as soon as we walk in with a surprised look on his face.

"Olivia, Alex, what brings you here?" he asks, his tone friendly but guarded.

"We need to talk to you, Jack," Alex says, shaking slightly.

Jack's expression turns serious, and I know he's ready for a storm from us. "Okay, take a seat."

We all sit on the sofa. I take a deep breath, trying to calm my nerves. Then I ask, "We heard about the French movie project falling through. And we heard that Jeff, the main investor, pulled out. What happened?"

Chapter 18. Jack

Olivia and Alex are sitting across from me. Their faces are stern and severe. I can sense their suspicion.

"What will you do if I've done something underhanded with the business?" I ask, glancing at both of their faces.

The room is quiet. The air is frozen.

Then Olivia looks up at me and says, "I will help you to make it right."

Alex agrees. "Yes, Jack, we'll help you to make it right."

My favorite director and my Olivia don't trust me. It's a joke to me. But I'm glad they haven't planned to leave me.

"Look, I know the rumors that are going around, but I want to clarify that I have never cheated in my business or personal life," I say firmly.

Olivia raises an eyebrow. "Then why did Jeff withdraw his investment from our project?"

"I don't know yet, but I'll find out," I reply.

Alex leans forward. "Jack, should we keep moving forward on the project?"

I nod. "Yes."

"Anything I can help with?" Alex asks.

"Fulfill your duties as a good director. I'll find the money." My voice is firm. I don't need Alex to be involved in this mess. Olivia and Alex exchange a look, but they are reassured by my words.

"How will you handle the situation?" Olivia asks with concern.

"I have a plan, but I can't tell you," I reply with a smile.

"Why?" Olivia asks.

"You'll share my plan with Sarah after you walk out this door, and Alex will become too nervous to do his job." I stand up, "Alex and Olivia, thank you for your concern. Next time, I wish you both could trust me more." I open the door and send them away.

I must resolve the problem before executing the final contract with my partner in France.

I pick up my phone and dial the number of the best private detective I know—Mr. Smith. The phone rings a few times before he answers.

"Hello, this is Mr. Smith," he says in a deep and authoritative voice.

"Hello, Mr. Smith, this is Jack. I need your help," I say, trying to sound as composed as possible.

"Of course, Jack. What do you need?" he asks.

"I need you to find out why Mr. Jeff Chesson, the banker who was supposed to invest in my project, suddenly stopped his investment," I explain.

"Consider it done, Jack. I'll start investigating right away," he replies confidently. "But we need to sign a contract first. My rate is $500 per hour."

"Deal." My voice is deep and firm.

I contact my partner in France, and he agrees to amend the contract. It will allow me ten more days to get the funds ready.

Ten days!

This is the deadline for me to fix my problem. Each day counts.

On day one, Mr. Smith stops by my office and collects all the necessary information. He is a thin man with intelligent eyes, very tall, and talks sharply.

On day two, no news.

On day three in the afternoon, I start thinking I could use my own money to fund the project in the worst-case scenario. It is my Plan B. While I think about my plan B, Mr. Smith calls me with some information.

"Hi, Jack. I have found out some interesting details about Jeff," he says.

"What did you find out?" I ask, eager to know the truth.

"First of all, Jeff has been facing some financial difficulties lately. He's been investing heavily in risky ventures overseas and losing money," Mr. Smith reveals.

"That's not good news," I mutter, feeling a sense of dread.

"Jeff has a connection with one of your directors. His name is Daniel."

"What did you find?" I have an awful feeling about what I just heard.

"They had a meeting today in Starbucks near your studio from 12:30 to 1:15 p.m. Daniel showed Jeff some paperwork. I passed by and pretended to pick up napkins. It looks like a business proposal. But I'm not sure about it. They discussed some profit margins. That's all I could hear," Mr. Smith says.

"How do you know it's Daniel?" I want to confirm the information has no mistakes.

"That's easy. The big fool was wearing his name tag." Mr. Smith laughs loudly at another end.

"It's progress, thank you. Please dig more into both Daniel and Jeff. I need to know if they made any deals behind my back."

I walk to the window, look at the blue sky, and green grass. I feel much better now. I already know the cause of my problem. I just need to verify it before acting.

The following two days I'm swamped with work. On day six in the morning, I realize I am still waiting to hear updates from Mr. Smith.

Now, I'm only four days away from the deadline. I already have my money ready. *I may have to use Plan B;* I think as I prop my feet on my desk and sip my coffee.

Olivia and I go to her pregnancy checkup appointment in the afternoon. We arrive at the doctor's office and check in at the front desk. Olivia is nervous, but I hold her hand tightly and reassure her that everything will be okay.

We're called into the ultrasound room, and Olivia lies on the bed while the technician prepares the equipment. The room is quiet, and the only sound is the soft hum of the ultrasound machine.

As the technician begins the exam, I look at the screen and see the tiny fetus for the first time. The fetus is about four months now, and I am amazed at how small it is, but at the same time, I feel a sense of wonder and joy. Suddenly, I see a movement on the screen, and the fetus seems to wave at us.

"Look!" I exclaim, pointing to the screen. "The baby is moving!"

Olivia turns her head to look at the screen and gasps. "Oh my God, it's moving!" she says, tears welling up in her beautiful eyes.

I feel a lump in my throat and a warm feeling in my chest. This is the first time I have ever seen my baby move, and it's a magical moment.

I can't believe that I'm going to be a father. I'm filled with a sense of pride and happiness, and I feel like I am on top of the world.

The technician continues to move the wand around, and we see more movement from the fetus. It's as if the baby is dancing inside of Olivia's womb. I can't help but smile and feel grateful for this moment.

After the ultrasound, the doctor comes in to discuss the exam results with us. Olivia is healthy, and the baby is growing normally. We both feel relieved and hug each other tightly.

As we leave the doctor's office, I can't stop thinking about the ultrasound and the joy of seeing my baby move for the first time. I feel a responsibility and love for my child, and I will do anything to ensure they have a happy and healthy life.

As I hold Olivia's hand and walk to the car, I receive a call from Mr. Smith. I let Olivia get into the car first.

"Hi, Jack, today I followed Daniel and found him driving to the Hilton Hotel at three o'clock. He walked into room 202, and about ten minutes later, a beautiful young lady entered the same room. It's been two hours and they're still inside."

"Do you have a photo of the lady?" I ask.

"Sure thing, I'll send it to you now." Mr. Smith sounds delighted.

Soon, Emily's photo shows up on my phone screen. She was walking in the hotel hallway, dressed in a sexy skirt. A beautiful snake.

When I finish my call and get into the car, Olivia asks, "Who's calling?"

"A coworker," I reply, pretending it's nothing important.

"How about Alex's project?" Olivia hands me a bottle of water she just got from the cooler.

"Fine." I take the water bottle and give Olivia a kiss. I don't want to leak anything to her. Olivia is a lovely girl but too nice to protect herself. "Olivia, pick your favorite restaurant. We'll go eat," I suggest.

"How about we go shopping first? I want to select baby clothes with you." Olivia smiles sweetly.

"Sure. We'll head to the mall. Let's go."

As we walk through the baby clothing section, I feel a headache coming on. I don't know what to pick, so I simply follow Olivia.

Suddenly, I hear a familiar voice. "Jack, what are you doing here?"

It's Paul. He seems surprised.

"I'm shopping," I reply, gesturing to Olivia, who is browsing through the racks of tiny clothes with a bright smile.

Paul nods slowly, his eyes darting between Olivia and me. "I see," he finally says. "Well, it's good to see you both."

Olivia turns to us and greets Paul and Jane with enthusiasm. She starts chatting with Jane about baby clothes and nursery decorations. They hit it off right away.

Paul stays quiet for a while, observing us from a distance. I can sense that he is still processing that I'm here with Olivia, and his face reveals a hint of worry and confusion.

After a few minutes of small talk, Jane excuses herself to go to the restroom, leaving Paul alone with us.

"Jack, can we talk?" Paul asks, his tone serious.

"Sure, what's up?" I reply, curious about what he wants to say.

Paul takes a deep breath before speaking. "Look, I know I haven't been the most supportive brother when it comes to you and Olivia, but I want you to know that I've been doing some thinking, and I realize that I've been unfair to you both."

I'm taken aback by his words. I've never seen Paul so vulnerable before.

"I've been too judgmental and quick to make assumptions about you and your intentions with Olivia," Paul admits. "I know now that you truly care for her and want to be a good father to our niece or nephew."

"Nephew, Paul!" I cry out loudly. Paul is finally coming around to our relationship. "Thank you, Paul," I say, touching his shoulder. "That means a lot to me."

Paul nods, looking at me intently. "But there's something else I need to talk to you about," he says, his voice serious again. "I've heard some rumors about your business dealings. Olivia told me that's not true. I trust you." Paul opens his arms and gives me a hug. "Let me know if you need me. We're family now."

"Thank you, brother!" I say sincerely.

Olivia is standing nearby and listening to the conversations between Paul and me. When she sees Paul hug me, she starts crying. Tears spill down her face, and she screams like a little girl.

Paul stands there and doesn't know what to do. Jane comes back in time. She smiles at Paul. "Olivia is relieved now. We should feel happy for her." Jane walks to Olivia and puts her arm on Olivia's shoulders. Soon, they're smiling together.

Paul says, "Let's go to a restaurant. My treat—a good meal as an apology."

"Great." I give Paul a high five. We have happy hour at the restaurant. It has been a while since I've shared much time with Paul.

As we leave the restaurant, Olivia gazes up at the full moon and turns to me. "Do you want to go to the park and look at the moon together?"

I smile, taking her hand. "I'd love to."

"Which Park?" I ask when we get into the car.

"The one where we had our night together," Olivia says quietly.

Her words bring me mixed feelings.

We walk around the park, enjoying the fresh night air and the calm atmosphere. The moon is big and bright in the sky, casting a silver glow over everything.

Olivia leads me to a bench under a tall tree, facing the lake. We sit down and gaze at the water, the sounds of crickets and frogs filling the air.

"It's beautiful," Olivia says softly.

I nod. "It is. I'm glad we came."

We sit silently for a few moments, taking in the peaceful scene around us. Then Olivia turns to me, her expression softening.

"Jack, I just wanted to say thank you for being here for me. I know it's not easy to manage all the drama with my brother and everything else that's going on, like Alex's project. But you've been so supportive and understanding. I appreciate it more than words can express."

I take her hand and give it a gentle squeeze. "Of course, Olivia. You know I'll always be here for you, no matter what."

She smiles warmly at me, her eyes shining in the moonlight. "I feel so lucky to have you in my life."

I lean in and kiss her, feeling grateful and content.

As we pull apart, Olivia turns back to the lake and sighs contentedly. "It's nights like this that make me realize how much I have to be grateful for."

I wrap my arm around her and rest my chin on her shoulder. "Me too," I say softly.

We sit there for a while longer, simply enjoying each other's company and the beauty of the night. Then I realize this was the spot where I had made love with her before.

I can see the love and happiness in her eyes. I feel ashamed of my past behavior, and I want to apologize.

"Olivia, I'm sorry for how I acted before," I say, my voice filled with regret.

"It's okay, Jack." Olivia replies, her voice calm and reassuring.

"I know, but I still feel guilty. I was a monster to you, and I don't deserve your forgiveness," I say, feeling the weight of my past actions on my shoulders.

Olivia takes my hand and squeezes it gently. "Jack, it's not about deserving forgiveness. It's about moving forward and being better." She kisses my hand and says, "Jack, I want you to be a free man in front of me. No apology between us."

I nod, understanding her words.

Olivia smiles at me, her eyes shining with love.

The moonlight casts a beautiful glow over the lake, the trees rustle in the gentle breeze, and our souls merge.

"I'm so excited to be a father," I say, breaking the silence.

Olivia's face lights up with joy. "Me too. I can't wait to meet our little one."

I take her hand in mine and place it on my chest. "I promise to be the best father I can be, Olivia. I will always be here for you and our child. We will have a happy family."

Olivia leans her head on my shoulder, and I wrap my arm around her. "Jack, you have broken all your rules," she says softly.

Contentment washes over me. I realize I'm no longer the same man who treated Olivia like a toy. I am now a man who has learned the value of love, respect, and commitment. I am a man who is ready to be a father and a loving partner.

"Jack, we can go. I need to shoot five scenes tomorrow. The director wants to complete the last of my shots in a week," Olivia says.

"I told him to do so. You're already four months pregnant, soon your body shape will change."

As we stand up, one thought suddenly comes to my mind: tomorrow will be day seven, and we are only three days away from needing to send the funds.

Will Mr. Smith bring me more news tomorrow?

Chapter 19. Olivia

The soft lighting fills Jack's bedroom with warmth. I lie quietly on the comfortable bed, waiting for his arrival. Jack's kind-heartedness has been restraining his desire with tenacious perseverance. He fears that making love will hurt the baby or me. While Jack is in the shower, I hide his pajamas. Tonight, I'm going to let Jack loose and be satisfied again.

Jack comes out of the bathroom wrapped in a white towel. Jack's body is as masculine as his personality. With his tyrant's mask removed, he has an extremely gentle and kind heart.

I'm fascinated both by his toughness and his gentleness.

"Jack, I want you tonight," I say as he approaches the bed.

Jack freezes for a moment. He did not expect my demand.

"You have a lot of work to do tomorrow." Jack bends to turn off the lamp.

"I understand. I just need a warm-up for tomorrow's work." I remove the towel from his body and expose him entirely to the light.

"Don't move. Let me take a good look at you." I press down on Jack's hand as he reaches for the light switch. It is the first time I have seen Jack's entire body clearly. His handsome face is sharp, and his bright eyes cannot hide his wisdom even in such tender moments; in his broad shoulders, arms, and slender legs, I can see strong muscles, just like a resurrected Spartan soldier.

"Okay, Jack, now you can turn off the lamp."

Jack stares at me with bright eyes and asks earnestly, "Are you sure I can turn off the lamp now?"

"I'm sure," I reply in the affirmative.

"No. It's not fair," Jack says, throwing off the thin fleece blanket I'm covered with. "Let me take a good look at you too. See what our little son has done to you."

Jack sits on the edge of the bed and gently unbuttons my pajamas.

His eyes first rest on my breasts. He smiles slightly. I know that he must have seen the changes in my body. My nipples have grown, and the areolas have turned from light to darker pink. My breasts have also become swollen. His gaze begins to move down and lands on my lower abdomen. My lower abdomen is slightly swollen, but fortunately, I am slim. It's hard to tell that I'm four months pregnant.

Then Jack put his face gently on my lower abdomen, trying to feel the slight fetal movement. He raises his head and says with disappointment, "During the ultrasound, I clearly saw that this guy would move. Why can't I feel it?"

"He's too young, and I only get slight movements sometimes. It's like a tickle," I explain. I turn off the light.

It is dark inside the bedroom now. In the dark, I become brave.

"Jack, I want you," I demand. I feel Jack's kiss on my cheek. It is a very tender kiss. "It's not like that. No. I want you to have me completely. I want you to relax completely," I add.

Jack lies down next to me. I feel his rapid breathing on my cheek. We kiss gently. I secretly wonder again why this tough guy's lips are so soft. My breasts feel the touch of his hands, powerful but very gentle. Jack masters pressure very well, sometimes just touching them separately, sometimes pushing them to the center of my chest, kissing them. Then Jack's hand begins to gently caress my abdomen and lower. When his fingers touch my clitoris, my whole body feels indescribable pleasure and desire for him. Jack continues to probe inside me with his fingers. It is the first time he has done so. He is constantly exploring, and his every movement is cautious.

My breathing becomes rapid.

Jack stands by the bed, turning me around so I can face him. He gently spreads my legs and places them over his shoulders. Then I feel his penetration.

He pushes very slowly, and I can clearly feel his depth. I cooperate with him with all my body and mind. It's a prolonged and tender lovemaking. We climax repeatedly. Strong Jack makes me feel out of body time and time again. Finally, I fall asleep in Jack's arms.

The following morning the sun shines bright as I walk into Jack's kitchen. I hug Jack from behind. "Good morning," I say.

"Morning," Jack says and puts the eggs into the pan.

"Jack, have you found out why Jeff stopped investing in your project?" I ask after sipping my coffee, hoping to get some insight into his progress.

"Olivia, I don't want to discuss it with you." Jack's tone is sharp as he dismisses the topic.

"Jack, I promise I won't leak it to anyone, even Paul. I'm worried about you."

Jack glances at me without a word. Jack's phone rings as we sit down to eat, interrupting our meal. He glances at the caller ID, then turns to me, "It is the detective I hired." Jack puts the phone on speaker so I can hear the conversation.

"Mr. Smith, what's the news?" Jack asks.

"Good morning to you too, Jack. I have some interesting news for you." The detective chuckles.

Jack leans forward. "Go on."

"Jack, guess what I found?"

From his joyful voice, I know he must have found something helpful; I quietly drop my fork onto my plate and lean closer to the phone.

"Tell me, please." Jack requests.

"I found Todd." Mr. Smith's voice is loud.

"Who is Todd? Todd, who?" Jack's voice is very demanding.

"Since Emily met Daniel in the hotel, I've been following Emily. Yesterday afternoon she met a big guy in LaLa's restaurant. They hugged and kissed in the parking lot. When they went inside, I checked on the big guy's car. There were some letters left on the passenger seat. Guess what I found?"

"Important information, of course," Jack urges shortly.

"His name is Todd Chesson."

"The same last name as Jeff?" Jack raises his voice.

"Yes!" Mr. Smith says.

"Are they related?" Jack asks.

"I'll find out how," Mr. Smith says confidently. "Jack, Todd has a lot of debts. Those papers are collection letters."

"It has become more interesting now," Jack says.

The detective chuckles again. "Jack, it's a small world. I'll dig and see what else I can find out."

Jack nods. "I need to know everything. Keep me updated."

As he hangs up, Jack turns to me with a serious expression. "Looks like our investigation just got a little more interesting."

I nod, feeling a thrill of excitement. "What do you think it means?"

"We'll see," Jack says. "But it's definitely worth looking into."

We finish breakfast in a few minutes, then head to the studio separately.

After arriving at the studio, I dive straight into shooting my scenes. The director is in high spirits, and the crew is efficient. We work quickly and smoothly, and before I know it, we're on to the film's last scene.

James calls for action, and I step into character.

I'm back in my hometown of Boston, walking in Harvard Square with my boyfriend—the former German officer, now working as a US spy.

As we walk hand in hand, we talk about our past and our hopes for the future. It's a tender and romantic moment, and I try to infuse my performance with the longing my character feels.

"Cut!" the director calls out. "Great job, everyone. Let's take a break and come back in ten minutes."

I take a deep breath and step out of character, feeling a sense of relief and satisfaction. I'm greeted by the rest of the cast and crew. We chat and joke around, enjoying the camaraderie of working on a film set. But for now, I'm just grateful to be a part of this incredible production, working with such a talented and dedicated cast and crew.

Ten minutes later, James stands in front of us. His voice is overly excited as he says, "We made it. All the scenes are canned. Congratulations and thanks to everyone."

Everyone on set starts yelling.

It's been a long journey, but we've made it to the end. I can feel the emotions bubbling up inside of me. Relief, joy, and a sense of accomplishment.

After the scene wraps, the crew cheers and applauds. I take a bow, feeling grateful for the experience and proud of the work we have done.

But as I leave the set and get coffee, my mind starts wandering. I think about Jack and the message I received from the detective this morning. Why is Emily dating Todd? And is Todd the same guy who followed me in the mall? I remember the detective used "big guy" to describe Todd. The guy who followed me was enormous and tall.

The questions keep swirling around in my head, and I can feel a sense of unease building up inside of me.

I walk back to the building and pick a quiet corner where no one can hear what I say. I call Jack.

Jack picks up on the first ring. "Hey, what's up?" he asks.

"I just finished shooting my last scene," I say.

"Hey, congratulations." Jack sounds delighted. "It's your first feature film."

"But I can't stop thinking about that message from the detective this morning," I say, and my voice is not too pleasant. "Jack, I want to find out if Todd is the same guy who followed me in the mall."

Jack sputters, "Easy. Let me ask the detective to send me a photo. I'll get back to you soon."

I follow the path, taking in the beautiful flowers around the buildings and waiting for Jack's message.

About eight minutes later, a text message pops up on my phone. It's Todd's photo. The shirt is different shirt, but still, his outfit is black from top to bottom. I call Jack. "Todd is the guy who followed me in the mall."

Jack is silent for a moment; I know he must be thinking hard. I feel a shiver running down my spine. The idea that Todd has been following me is unsettling, to say the least. Who knows what they could do next.

"Do you think we should go to the police?" I ask.

"Not yet," Jack says. "We don't have enough evidence to go to them just yet. But I'm going to keep working on it. In the meantime, be careful and keep your eyes open."

I nod even though Jack can't see me. "Okay."

We hang up and I'm left with my thoughts again.

The rest of the day goes by in a blur as I pack up my things and say goodbye to the cast and crew. But all the while, my mind is racing with questions and concerns.

Night arrives and I can't sleep. I toss and turn, thinking about Todd and Emily and their connection. I try to rationalize it—it's all just a coincidence. But deep down, I know that something isn't right.

I wish Jack could be home with me, but Jack is working outside, leaving me alone in this big house. I hold Jack's pillow and fall asleep.

I wake up with a start, drenched in sweat. Jack's arms are around me. My heart is pounding in my chest, and it takes a bit to remember where I am. Then I hear Jack calling me. "Olivia, are you okay?"

"Jack, I had a nightmare. A horrible one." The nightmare has left me shaken and scared.

I can't shake the image of Todd's face or the feeling of the elevator falling endlessly. And the laughter—was it really Emily's voice?

"Olivia, what was your nightmare?" Jack asks, his voice concerned.

I describe my dream to Jack.

I find myself standing in a shopping mall. The air is thick with the smell of perfume and the sound of chatter and laughter, but I cannot see anyone.

I'm unsure why I'm here, but I start walking, aimlessly wandering from store to store. As I walk, I sense unease building up inside me. I want to leave, but I can't find the way out. It's then that I see the elevator. It's one of those old-fashioned ones with metal grilles and a manual door that slides shut. Without thinking, I step inside. But as soon as the door closes, I realize something is wrong. A man is standing in the corner, facing the wall. I can't see his face, but I can feel his presence. As the elevator starts moving, the man turns around. It's Todd. I try to get out, but the door won't budge. I'm trapped inside, hurtling toward my doom. The elevator starts falling, faster and faster, endless. I can feel my stomach drop as we plummet toward the ground. Todd is laughing, both hands holding a sharp knife. The laughter changes, becoming a woman's voice. It's Emily. I can see her standing on top of the elevator shaft, watching me fall and die. I try to scream, but no sound comes out. I'm trapped, helpless, and alone.

As we near the bottom, I can see the ground rushing to meet me. I brace for impact; there's no way to escape.

But just as the elevator is about to crash, I wake up, drenched in sweat and gasping for breath.

The nightmare lingers, haunting me even as I try to shake it off. Being trapped and helpless, the feeling of falling endlessly—it's all too real.

"Olivia, you are not alone, not helpless. I'm your protector." Jack's voice is steadfast and confident. "I'll not allow anyone to hurt you."

Jack's words make me feel much better. As I try to calm myself down, I wonder what it all means. Is it a warning? A premonition? Or is it just my subconscious playing tricks on me?

Chapter 20. Jack

Now I have two days to settle the funding for Alex's project. Last night, Olivia's nightmare, is still alive in my mind. I must protect her at all costs.

My office door shut. Jay, my assistant, cannot hear the conversation in this room. The morning light shines on the photos and papers spread across my desk. I haven't touched them yet.

I sit across from Mr. Smith. I look into his sharp eyes, my tone stern as he lays out the facts.

"So, what you're saying is that Jeff had a son named Todd with a married woman twenty-six years ago?" I ask, leaning forward in my chair.

"Exactly," the detective confirms, "The woman gave birth to Todd and put him up for adoption. Jeff and Todd only reconnected three years ago."

I nod, taking it all in. It's a bombshell revelation that could have severe consequences for Jeff and his family.

"And what about Emily?" I ask, my voice cold and calculated. "What does she have to do with all of this?"

The detective grins, his humor breaking through the tension. "Well, it turns out that Emily is a drug dealer. She sells drugs to Todd. And after she found out that Todd is Jeff's son, she started giving him product for free."

I sneer contemptuously. So, I still underestimated Emily. Her actions are not only illegal but also reckless and dangerous.

"What did you find about Daniel?" I ask.

"Well, Daniel showed Jeff his project can be more commercially successful than yours."

"How did you find all this out?" I ask.

"I have my ways." Mr. Smith wants to keep his secrets. "But I can tell you in detail about what I found." He smiles.

"Fair enough," I say.

"Emily introduced Daniel to Todd and asked Todd to refer Daniel to Jeff," the detective begins.

I nod. It sounds logical. "And what happened next?" I keep digging.

"Well, Daniel offered Jeff a project with a higher profit margin than the one you had offered him. About 5% higher, to be exact."

I smile.

I had already offered Jeff the best deal he could get in this industry. When Daniel says he can get him an unrealistic rate of return, he can only have one of two results: he breaks his business or breaks his promise.

The detective continues. "Daniel then tried to switch Jeff to invest in his project instead."

"Did Jeff go for it?" I ask.

The detective nods grimly. "Sure thing, Jeff did. He will sign the contract whenever Daniel jumps out to collaborate with a different producer. Daniel is leaving you. And to sweeten the deal, Daniel offered to kick back 1% of the net profit to Todd."

My blood boils at the thought of Daniel's underhanded tactics. But I'm glad Daniel will leave, so I don't have to kick him out.

"Well done, Mr. Smith. Thank you very much for all your help," I say, sending him on his way.

I know it is time to call Paul, not as my best friend but as an intelligent businessperson.

I dial Paul's number, feeling a sense of urgency. He answers on the second ring.

"Hey, Jack," he says, his voice casual.

"Paul, I need to talk to you about something important," I explain, my voice serious.

There is a brief pause before he says, "Okay, shoot."

I take a deep breath and summarize all the information the detective found out about Daniel and his unethical business practices. I recount the story, explaining how Daniel convinced Jeff to invest in his project instead.

"So, what are you going to do about it?" Paul asks.

"I need to get funds ready in two days," I admit, "though I have a plan B. I can invest my own money."

"Jack, what will you do with your money if you don't have to active plan B?"

"I'll invest in a new studio in New York. I already planned for it," I reply. I hope to still invest in the New York studio. It will take my business to a higher level.

Paul's voice is calm. "Okay, well, let's figure out our next steps. Can you email me the proposal? I want to look and see if there's anything I can do."

"Thanks, Paul," I say gratefully. "I really appreciate your support."

"Of course, man," he replies. "We're best friends, remember? We stick together through thick and thin."

I smile at his words, feeling gratitude for our friendship. Paul has always been there for me through good times and bad. I know I can count on him to have my back.

As soon as we hang up, I email the proposal to him.

Then I wait for Paul's response. Time suddenly becomes so slow.

Four hours later, Paul calls me back. "Okay, I've gone through your proposal. Your numbers make sense. I like it, and I have an idea," he says excitedly.

"Tell me," I say.

"Well, I can invest 30%, and two of my investors will invest 70%. They've been collaborating with me for years. Anything I have skin in, they will join for sure. Together, we'll replace Jeff."

"Great." I stand up from my chair. "That will free me to continue my investment in the New York studio." I feel a renewed determination.

After finishing the call with Paul, I feel hungry and realize I haven't had my lunch. Before ordering my meal, I must call Olivia. I must tell her this good news, so she doesn't have to worry about me.

"Olivia," I say, my voice excited. "Paul found the funds for Alex's project."

"That's great, Jack. I'm so lucky to have both of you," Olivia shouts happily.

A light knock on the door interrupts my conversation with Olivia, and my assistant Jay walks in. "Boss, Nancy, the production manager, has something urgent to see you about."

After saying goodbye to Olivia, I tell Jay, "Please, send her in."

Nancy does not sit down. After making sure the office door is shut, she whispers, "Daniel is in trouble."

I look at Nancy without speaking. I wait silently for her to continue explaining the situation.

"He's in the police station now. Should we bail him out?"

"Please sit down." I point at a chair near my desk.

After Nancy sits down, I lean back in my chair and ask, "What did he do?"

"According to the police station, it was because of violence."

"How much is bail?"

"Fifty thousand dollars." Nancy's voice is nervous. The bail is costly.

"Who was beaten?" I am already making various guesses when I ask.

"I don't know," Nancy answers nervously, "Are we going to pay the bail?"

I glance at my watch. It's 2:40 in the afternoon. I tell Nancy, "Thank you, Nancy. Please write down the address and phone number of the police station, and I will take care of the rest. Do not tell anyone about this."

I arrive at the police station an hour later, feeling a mix of emotions.

As I enter the visiting room, I take in my surroundings. The room is small and sparsely furnished, with a few plastic chairs and a table in the center. The walls are a dull gray, and there's a small window high up on one wall, letting in a sliver of natural light.

I take a seat at the table and wait for Daniel to arrive. A few minutes later, he's escorted in by a police officer. He looks tired and disheveled, with dark circles under his eyes.

"Hey," he says, his voice hoarse. "Thanks for coming."

I nod, feeling a pang of sympathy for him. "What happened, Daniel? Why are you here?"

He takes a deep breath. "Last night I stopped by Emily's home, expecting a romantic night with her. I love her. But when I got there,

I found her and Todd on the bed, surrounded by drugs. I was angry she had betrayed me."

I listen carefully, trying to keep an open mind. "What happened next?"

"Todd kicked me hard, right in the stomach," he says, wincing at the memory. "I stumbled back, trying to catch my breath. And then, I don't know, something just snapped inside me. I grabbed the lamp and used it to hit Todd's head. He went down hard, and I thought he was dead. I called 9-1-1."

I feel a wave of shock and horror at his words. This is not the Daniel I know, the calm and collected businessman who always has a plan. This is someone else entirely, someone consumed by anger and desperation.

"What are you going to do now?" I ask.

He shakes his head, looking defeated. "I don't know. I've already messed up so much. I don't know if Emily will ever speak to me again."

"You still love her?" I ask.

"Yes, but she's in big trouble. Emily was arrested last night. The cops found drugs in her home. I have no idea what will happen to her."

Despite everything that had happened, I can still see the pain and regret in his eyes. I feel sympathy for him, but Daniel is not a wise man.

"Daniel, you need to take responsibility for your actions," I say firmly. "I'm not going to buy you out, but I'll find you a good lawyer. If all you told me is true and Todd started the fight, what you did is self-defense."

He nods, looking up at me with a glimmer of hope. "Thank you."

As I leave the visiting room, I feel sad and regretful. It's never easy to see someone you know going through such a grim time.

I call my attorney when I stop by the McDonald's drive through. I believe my attorney can get Daniel out for a few thousand dollars.

Two days later the studio is bustling with activity as I prepare for the big party. The air is filled with excitement, and I can feel my pulse racing.

The party is to celebrate Alex's fully executed project contract. It will be a world-class movie, and we all expect to see it come to life on the big screen. We're also celebrating the successful completion of James's film, which is the first feature movie for Olivia. It's a huge milestone for her, and we're all proud of her hard work and dedication.

As the guests arrive, I can see the excitement in their eyes. Paul and the other two investors for Alex's project are there, along with William, one of the investors. They are all in high spirits, eager to celebrate our success.

We sing, dance, and drink to our success, feeling a sense of camaraderie and community. The music is loud, the drinks are flowing, and everyone is happy. It is the first time I've danced with Olivia. Her face is pink, and she is extremely excited.

At the peak of the party, I ask everyone to be quiet. I leave Olivia in the center of the room. Then, with soft music playing, forty girls wearing pink mopping dresses walk in with red roses and surround Olivia. Olivia seems to have suddenly turned into a flower fairy, in the center of layers of roses.

In front of the surprised eyes of everyone, the girls holding flowers open a passage for me. I go to Olivia along the aisle, go down on one knee, and propose to her in front of everyone attending the party.

"Olivia, will you marry me?" My voice is loud and sincere.

Olivia looks stunned, but then a smile spreads across her face. "Yes," she says, her voice choked with emotion.

Then we hug and kiss.

Everyone cheers for us. I see Paul quietly wiping away the tears from the corners of his eyes.

I also see Daniel clapping for us. It's good he's still here with us, supporting us and celebrating our success. It is a reminder that there can be light and joy even amid the darkness.

As the night wears on, everyone is still cheerful.

Olivia grins, her eyes shining with joy. "Jack, I couldn't be happier."

I wrap my arms around her waist, feeling a sense of warmth and love. "Me too," I say softly. "I can't wait to spend the rest of my life with you."

She leans into me, her head resting against my chest. "I love you," she says, her voice soft and tender.

"I love you too," I reply, feeling a sense of contentment settle over me. I see Paul watching us with a smile on his face.

I take Olivia's hand and walk over to Paul.

"Dude, you still owe us a blessing," I demand loudly.

Paul opens his arms and hugs Olivia and me together. "I wish you love forever," he says, his voice full of emotion.

Special Offer

If you like this book, please read "***Twins For the Forbidden Billionaire***" by clicking here!

Signup for my newsletter to receive updates on upcoming releases and a GIFT by clicking here!

If you like this book, please leave a review on Amazon. It would be a tremendous help to me as an upcoming author.

Thank you so much for reading my book.

Love,

Lily

Printed in Great Britain
by Amazon

40870521R00108